The Secrets Of Colchester Hall

Sophie Barnes

Published by Sophie Barnes, 2021.

By Sophie Barnes
Novels

The Formidable Earl
Her Seafaring Scoundrel
The Forgotten Duke
More Than A Rogue
The Infamous Duchess
No Ordinary Duke
The Illegitimate Duke
The Girl Who Stepped Into The Past
The Duke of Her Desire
Christmas at Thorncliff Manor
A Most Unlikely Duke
His Scandalous Kiss
The Earl's Complete Surrender
Lady Sarah's Sinful Desires
The Danger in Tempting an Earl
The Scandal in Kissing an Heir
The Trouble with Being a Duke
The Secret Life of Lady Lucinda
There's Something About Lady Mary
Lady Alexandra's Excellent Adventure

SOPHIE BARNES

How Miss Rutherford Got Her Groove Back

Novellas

The Secrets of Colchester Hall
Once Upon a Townsbridge Story
An Unexpected Temptation
A Duke for Miss Townsbridge
Falling For Mr. Townsbridge
Lady Abigail's Perfect Romance
When Love Leads To Scandal
Miss Compton's Christmas Romance
The Duke Who Came To Town
The Earl Who Loved Her
The Governess Who Captured His Heart
Mistletoe Magic (from Five Golden Rings: A Christmas Collection)

Chapter One

Rivulets of water slid down the windowpane, blurring the view from the carriage. Jostling along the rutted country road, Angelica Florence Northbridge pressed her palm to the glass and peered out at the dreary wetness, hoping to catch a better glimpse of her destination. From what she'd seen so far, it did not look nearly as inviting as she had hoped.

Although she was a self-professed gothic novel enthusiast, there was a difference between reading about a bleak castle haunted by restless spirits and actually having to visit one. Not that Colchester Hall was rumored to house supernatural entities, but with black clouds hanging low and rain pelting down, the setting was perfect for an Anne Radcliffe story.

"Why did we have to come here?" Angelica asked her mother, Rose. "I would so much rather have remained at home."

"And done what exactly?" Rose inquired.

"Read?" Angelica suggested. "Work on my correspondence?"

"Both of which can be accomplished anywhere. And since Viscount Sterling was kind enough to extend an invitation to us, I thought it wise to accept."

What went unsaid was the fact that Rose desperately longed to see her youngest daughter settled. Angelica's four older sisters had all married in recent years, but with another Season come and gone, Angelica's future remained uncertain.

"Have you ever met him?" Angelica asked. The carriage rocked as it followed a curve in the road.

"Once. Before he married. His father attended Oxford with your papa."

A mournful silence followed. According to what Angelica had learned from her mother, Sterling had been only eight and twenty when his wife perished. Now, two years later, he was looking to re-marry. Any uncertainty regarding this had been dispelled by the blunt invitation. It had read as follows: *I am in need of a wife and your daughter could be a suitable candidate for the position. Please join me at my estate from September 10th to September 24th so we may determine our compatibility.*

In Angelica's opinion, the blunt order hadn't deserved a response, but of course her mother had disagreed. One could not snub a viscount. It simply wasn't done. And as tempted as Angelica had been to argue the point, she'd refrained because of her mother's clear desperation. With no other suitors forthcoming, the time for being picky had passed "What was your impression of him?" Angelica asked.

Rose sighed. "He was nice enough, I suppose."

With a roll of her eyes, Angelica muttered, "I can scarcely wait to meet him, Mother."

"Well, opinions are objective. I've always been wary of swaying those of others."

Angelica slumped against the squabs and glanced out toward the grey stone façade now filling her vision. "How annoyingly diplomatic of you."

Rose smiled. "You'll meet him soon enough and then you may judge for yourself." The carriage rolled to a swaying halt near the front steps of Colchester Hall. A footman holding an oiled silk umbrella opened the carriage door and helped Rose alight.

Careful to steer her around the puddles, he escorted her inside the manor before returning to offer Angelica his assistance. She made her way across the short expanse of gravel, climbed the wide steps, crossed the threshold...and froze.

"Goodness gracious." Judging from the dull exterior, she never would have dreamed Colchester Hall possessed a foyer so grand. Domed and three stories high, it seemed to stretch toward heaven, the walls and ceiling adorned by murals featuring colorful garlands carried by birds and angels. The paint was faded and even peeling in a few places, but that did not detract from the beauty. A sweeping stone staircase rose toward the first floor landing to join the balcony bordering the periphery of the room.

"Isn't it magnificent?" a breathy voice that wasn't Rose's asked.

Angelica lowered her gaze to a young lady with eyes so large and inquisitive they made her look slightly owlish. "It is indeed," Angelica said. She waited for the lady to introduce herself, but when she didn't, Angelica decided she would go first. "I'm Lady Angelica Northbridge. And you are?"

The young lady blinked. "Miss Lucinda Harlow, but um..." She shrugged. "You can call me Lucy."

Angelica instantly smiled in response to her timid yet friendly tone. "It's nice to make your acquaintance, Lucy. And please feel free to forgo the honorific with me as well"

Lucy offered a shy smile. "All right."

Unsure of what else to say, Angelica glanced around in search of her mother and found her chatting with another woman of similar age. Perhaps Lucy's mother? Or maybe she was chaperone to one of the other four ladies who'd piled into the foyer while Angelica had been busy staring up at the ceiling and introducing herself to Lucy,

"Do you suppose we're all here for the same reason?" Angelica asked Lucy under her breath. It had not occurred to her until then that Sterling would want to invite a selection of potential brides. She groaned at the prospect of having to compete – or rather of having her mother insist she do – against other women.

"Well," Lucy mumbled, barely loud enough for Angelica to hear, "I doubt they've come for the sake of the weather."

Angelica pinched her lips together to keep from laughing and decided right then and there that she and Lucy were going to get along splendidly. "Did your invitation allude to forming an attachment with the viscount?"

"Mm...hmm."

"Then we're here for precisely the same reason. To vie for his hand."

"I'd rather not," Lucy muttered.

Angelica felt much the same but knew it was too late to back out now. After all, they were here and if she didn't make an effort, she'd only upset her mother. Not to mention, she wasn't entirely sure what she'd do if she did not marry

7

*some*body. The last thing she wanted to be was a burden. Compared with that horrifying possibility, marriage seemed like a very acceptable outcome. And who knew? Perhaps Viscount Sterling would turn out to be the man of her dreams – a man with whom she could see herself falling hopelessly in love.

"And you are?"

Angelica stared at the haughty blonde who'd materialized before her for a good three seconds before recalling her manners and forcing a smile. "Lady Angelica Northbridge. And this is my friend, Miss Lucinda Harlow."

"I am Lady Seraphina." Her Haughtiness raised her chin just enough to stare down her nose at Angelica. "My father is the Duke of Guildenridge, which practically makes me royal." She tittered – *tittered* – like some shrill canary. And then the edge of her mouth tilted into a mocking caricature of a smile. "Well, it was lovely to meet you." She didn't spare Lucy one glance. "I'm sure we'll get to know each other better in the coming days." This was said with a hint of foreboding before she turned away.

"A duke's daughter," Lucy said with awe. "Why on earth would she ever consider marrying a viscount?"

Angelica snorted. "I suspect her winning personality and meekness must be to blame."

"What an awful thing to say." Lucy chuckled.

"Why? I didn't insult her."

"Yes you did."

Angelica supposed Lucy did have a point, but she was prevented from commenting further since Rose approached at that moment and promptly began introducing her to the remaining three ladies. Matilda Stevens was the only child of a wealthy landowner, Clare St. James was an orphan whose guardian was a baron, and Anna Chesterfield's father was untitled, though the second son of an earl. None said enough for Angelica to form much of an opinion on either of them.

She took a deep breath and shared a quick look of despair with her mother. For although she might have been rapidly approaching a state of spinsterhood, she never would have thought she deserved to be grouped with what appeared to be the least marriageable women on the market. It was harrowing, to be sure, and frankly quite sad. Worst of all was the prospect of having to prove she'd make the most suitable wife. Nothing appealed less.

All she wanted was to go home.

"Ah. I see you are all assembled," a breezy feminine voice said. It belonged to an elegant woman of slim build with a lovely face and hair that shone like gold. "I am Mrs. Essex, housekeeper to Lord Sterling and this..."

Angelica didn't hear anything else the woman said. She was too busy wondering how a young woman who looked as she did could possibly be a housekeeper to anyone.

"Angelica," Rose hissed right next to her ear.

"What?"

"Shall we follow Mrs. Essex upstairs so she can show us to our rooms?"

"Oh. Um. Isn't there a butler?"

Rose shook her head in dismay and gave Angelica's hand a tug. The rest of the party had started climbing the stairs while she'd been woolgathering. "Mrs. Essex just introduced him. He's the older gentleman over there issuing orders to the footmen. Clarkson is his name."

Angelica cast a glance toward the spot her mother indicated and instantly found the man to whom she referred. Gray hair and a serious demeanor, she noted with some satisfaction. He fit his role so much better than Mrs. Essex did hers.

"Dinner will be served at precisely seven o'clock," Mrs. Essex told Angelica once she'd shown her to her room. Apparently the mansion was large enough to allow each guest a room of her own so Angelica wouldn't have to share with her mother.

Instead...

She turned and allowed her mouth to fall open. The room she'd been given was at least twice the size of the one she had at home. Furnished in pretty cream tones accented by soft shades of blue, it was, quite literally, perfect.

With a satisfied sigh she stepped farther into the room. Her trunk had been placed at the foot of the canopy bed, and a maid was already busy unpacking it. Angelica thanked the girl and went to peer out the window. Water streaked over the glass but she could still make out a series of walkways leading toward a pavilion. Strategically placed statues and benches offered further evidence of a well-planned garden, although it didn't look terribly inviting in the rain.

"Good heavens. Your room is at least twice the size of mine."

Angelica turned from the window, ignored the shiver blowing over her shoulders, and smiled at Lucy. "Really?" She rubbed her hands together and moved closer to the fireplace. "I would have imagined all the guestrooms to be the same size."

"They used to be." Mrs. Essex said. She'd somehow materialized directly behind Lucy, causing her to jump.

"Goodness," Lucy gasped, her hand pressed to her breast. "I didn't realize you were there."

Mrs. Essex gave an indulgent smile. "Forgive me. It was not my intention to startle you." She approached Angelica. "I believe your mother is freshening up, so I chose not to disturb her. But I thought it prudent to inform you that you can use this connecting door over here to access her room more directly. If you wish."

Angelica hadn't even noticed the door since it was located behind a screen that separated the dressing area and toilette from the rest of the room. Tilting her head, she considered the convenience. "How unusual." She glanced at Mrs. Essex. "For guestrooms, I mean, to be joined in such a manner. I'm assuming there must be a key, because otherwise it—"

"Of course there is. I have it right here." Mrs. Essex handed an ornately fashioned brass key to Angelica. "But you're right. It is unusual." She inhaled deeply while giving the room a full perusal, then said, "If you must know, this used to be her ladyship's room. Your mother has the viscount's former bedchamber."

"I...see," Angelica murmured. Another shiver raked the length of her spine, like fingernails scraping her skin. She instinctively glanced over her shoulder, but of course, no one was there.

"The viscount decided to move to the opposite side of the castle a couple of years ago."

Angelica stared at her. She then glanced at Lucy, whose eyes had grown to the size of saucers. As if reading her mind, Angelica let her gaze wander across the room until it settled on the bed. She swallowed. And then, because she simply had to know, she quietly asked, "Did the late viscountess, um... Did she..."

"No," Mrs. Essex said. "She did not die in that bed." Angelica breathed a sigh of relief. The housekeeper smiled, perhaps with reassurance or perhaps with a touch of wistfulness. "She froze to death outside. Beneath that very window."

Lucy gasped.

A tremor swept through Angelica's body and she instinctively turned. A gentle movement caught the corner of her eye – the curtain perhaps. A draft could have stirred it, she reasoned. Or there might have been nothing at all except for her own overactive imagination.

"Well, then. I do believe I'll let you get settled," Mrs. Essex announced in a cheerful tone. "Please use the bell pull if you need anything else and feel free to explore the downstairs at your leisure. Just be sure to stay out of the east wing. His lordship likes to keep that part of the house private." She spoke a few extra words to the maid, who appeared to be nearly done with unpacking Angelica's things. One minute later, both had departed, leaving Angelica alone with Lucy.

"She's a bit odd, don't you think?" Lucy asked with a quick backward glance as if to make sure Mrs. Essex wouldn't suddenly pop up behind her.

"Very," Angelica murmured. "I can't imagine the future Lady Sterling wanting to keep her on. She's far too young and pretty."

"It all depends on what his lordship is like, I suppose. Perhaps he has kept Mrs. Essex in his employ for intimate reasons." She gave Angelica a pointed look.

Angelica felt her lips twitch. "You've quite a wicked mind for someone who's so soft spoken."

"Well, I might not be outgoing, but that doesn't stop my brain from working. And don't tell me you haven't had the same notion."

Of course she had. Her mother had always been shockingly forthright with her, for, as she liked to say, knowledge was power and ignorance only led to bad choices. So Angelica knew what went on between men and women behind closed doors, and she knew it was common for some men to keep a mistress.

Angelica rolled her eyes at her own wayward thoughts and shook her head. There was obviously a Mr. Essex and shame on her anyway for immediately thinking the worst just because the woman didn't fit the typical housekeeper mold.

"Come on," Angelica told Lucy as she grabbed a shawl and wrapped it around her shoulders. "I'm sure there must be a library. Let's go find it, shall we?"

They checked with both of their mothers first just to let them know where they were off to. "We'll order some tea," Angelica said as they walked down the stairs. She pulled her shawl tighter to ward off the chill creeping up the back of her neck. Good lord, it was only September, yet it felt like the middle of winter. Which was reason enough for her not to marry Lord Sterling. In spite of its grandeur, Colchester Hall was felt a huge mausoleum, and she could not see herself living here.

RAISING A SNIFTER OF brandy to his lips, Randolph Benedict Scott Trevarian took a long swallow and savored the hot burn that followed. Inviting six debutantes to his home for the sake of selecting one as his future viscountess had been his idea alone. He had no one to blame for their presence but himself. Yet he'd started to have some serious doubts about the sanity of his decision since their arrival, because now he had to entertain them. At the very least, he should have asked some of his married friends to attend the house party as well, for the sake of balance and, perhaps, moral support.

But he'd had no such brilliant notion until this second and now it was too late. He was alone as host and gentleman with six expectant young ladies and their eager chaperones to contend with. He glanced at the clock. It was almost six thirty. He took another sip of his drink, aware that he ought to go down and greet his guests as they gathered for dinner.

A knock at the door offered a welcome delay.

"Enter!"

Mrs. Essex glided into his study. She was, he'd noted a long time ago when she'd first begun in his employ, exceptionally pretty, although there was something about her – a flawlessness – he found strangely unappealing. Nevertheless, it had surprised him that his wife had hired her, but she'd been confident in his faithfulness and insisted they help the poor woman who'd recently lost her husband.

Now here they were, a widow and widower beneath the same roof. He had no doubt some of the other servants wondered if they'd become lovers. And Randolph was man enough to admit to having considered it on occasion, if only for a fleeting second. For although he knew most men would probably let themselves be tempted by the lovely Mrs. Essex, he wasn't really attracted to her at all. Never had been. And even if he were, he was not the sort of man who'd ever proposition a servant, no matter how high ranking she might be.

"Since you're the only gentleman here, I thought you might like to forego the after dinner drink in your study and take tea with the ladies instead," Mrs. Essex said with a warm and inviting smile. "It will allow you to further your acquaintance with them in a less formal setting."

"How thoughtful." Randolph set his glass aside and met her gaze directly. "What is your opinion of them so far?"

"I really can't say."

"Can't or don't wish to?" He deliberately smiled in an effort to soften her up. "Come now, Mrs. Essex, I'd like to know what you think."

Mrs. Essex appeared to consider. Randolph glanced at the clock. He really should get going. "None," she eventually said.

"That's not very helpful."

"Perhaps not, but none of the ladies you have invited stand out." She shrugged one shoulder. "They're forgettable. Except for Lady Seraphina."

"Oh?" As she was the daughter of a duke, he'd wondered about her unmarried state. Surely men would be lining up outside her door?

Mrs. Essex actually grinned. "You'll see what I mean."

"Is she hideous?"

"My lord! What a thing to suggest."

"It is a reasonable assumption to make," he muttered. And it might not be the worst thing in the world, having a wife who would not tempt other men to her bed. It was, after all, why he'd asked these particular women to join him in the first place. Because each and every one had been unable to snatch up a husband.

"You should head toward the parlor now unless you wish to be late to your own dinner party. And I," she announced with a flourish, "must return to the kitchen to make sure everything runs smoothly."

"Mrs. Essex," he said, halting her in the middle of her departure. She glanced back with one raised eyebrow. "Thank you."

Her lips curved with pleasure. Her pale blue eyes gleamed as they caught the light from the oil lamp. She added a nod, and then she was gone. Randolph blew out a breath, gave his sleeves a quick tug and checked his cravat. Satisfied with his appearance, he made his way through the long oak-paneled hallway that would take him to the parlor adjoining the dining room.

Once there, he did not have to wait long before the first young ladies arrived with their mothers. Randolph stepped forward, hands clasped behind his back, and offered a partial bow to each of them in turn. "Good evening." He directed most of his attention to the two women he was meant to consider. "Viscount Sterling, at your service."

Both ladies curtsied and then their mothers introduced them as Miss Matilda Stevens and Miss Anna Chesterfield.

"A pleasure," Randolph told them politely. He barely managed to ask them about their journey before Miss Clare St. James arrived. She was the shortest of the three and the least attractive. She also seemed to speak solely in nods and head shakes, so if he meant to marry a woman with whom he could carry on conversations, he probably shouldn't consider her. Although, he reflected, there was a chance she was merely nervous, and it would be terribly ill-bred of him to judge her too quickly.

With this in mind, he deliberately said, "Tell me about your hobbies."

Her lips parted, she seemed to stammer something, though he'd no clue what, and then she shook her head and retreated until the back of her legs connected with a chair. She sat with the most terrified expression he'd ever seen on anyone's face.

Irritated, Randolph located her chaperone – a friend of her guardian's – and bluntly asked, "Is something the matter with her?"

"I'm terribly sorry, my lord, but she's painfully shy. Allow her a couple of days to adjust, and I'm sure she'll warm to you."

She warm to *him*?

It took no small effort for him to keep a straight face and not blurt out an insult. Instead, he managed a nod and decided to give his attention back to Miss Chesterfield and Miss Stevens. Only as he turned, he spotted a lady who'd just stepped through the door. Her poise was perfect, if a little aloof, but her face was pleasing enough to the eye, and there was a natural elegance about her that would suit a viscountess very well.

Their eyes met. Randolph's stomach tightened with anticipation. This could be his future wife. She raised her chin, drew back her shoulders, and smiled in a disconcertingly predatory way as she started toward him. Randolph tried not to be put off. After all, determination could be an admirable feature. But then she reached him and rather than say some polite words of greeting, she raised her right arm, stretching it out until her hand was almost level with his chin. And waited.

Randolph stared down at the back of her hand. Her motive could not have been more obvious if she'd been carrying a sign that read: You may have the pleasure of dropping a kiss right there.

One side of his lips curled upward with an almost dastardly sense of amusement. There had to be a little devil inside him, for rather than do as he ought and follow along with his guest's expectations, he reached up, grabbed her fingers at a somewhat awkward angle, and shook them.

"You must be Lady Seraphina," he said.

"I, um..." He could tell she was struggling to hide her outrage. "Yes." She smiled tightly. Her chaperone, who'd appeared at her side roughly ten seconds earlier, stared at him in wonder. Clearly, no one had ever thwarted this spoiled woman's will before.

Well, there was a first time for everything, Randolph decided. He dropped her hand unceremoniously and looked past her shoulder, immediately spotting the two last remaining young ladies whom he'd invited. Lady Angelica and Miss Harlow had apparently seen enough of what had transpired between him and Lady Seraphina, for their hands were clapped over their mouths as if to hold back an onslaught of laughter.

Or perhaps to stop themselves from verbally assaulting him for his rudeness. It could be either, judging from their expressions.

He considered them. One blonde, one brunette, both slim and neither particularly pretty. At least not in the classical sense. He had no idea which was which. Perhaps it was time to find out? Ignoring Lady Seraphina's sputtering attempt to maintain a proper demeanor, he ambled over to where Lady Angelica and Miss Harlow stood with their mothers directly behind them.

"Thank you for coming," he said. "I am your host, Viscount Sterling."

"Delighted," one of the mothers said. "I am the dowager Lady Bloomfield and this is my daughter, Lady Angelica."

Lady Angelica, who'd dropped her hand to reveal a wide mouth with much fuller lips than he would have expected, watched him with sparkling eyes. To his surprise, his heart leapt a little when she smiled. Perhaps because the expression was genuine, completely devoid of pretense, and entirely focused on him – like they were co-conspirators with a shared secret. It was the oddest thing.

"A pleasure," he murmured, while holding her gaze. She might not be able to compete with Mrs. Essex where looks were concerned, but there was something about her, something he liked so much better than what most would describe as perfect beauty.

"And I am Mrs. Harlow," the other mother was saying. Randolph tore his gaze away from Lady Angelica so he could greet Miss Harlow as well.

"I trust your journeys to my corner of the world went well?" he inquired once the introductions had been completed and Lady Bloomfield and Mrs. Harlow had removed themselves to another part of the room.

"We did arrive unscathed," Lady Angelica said. "As you can see."

"Indeed."

"In spite of the rain," Miss Harlow added in a much softer voice than Lady Angelica used. Clearly, she was the more timid one of the two.

"Yes. I must confess that I did suggest we turn around more than once," Lady Angelica said without looking the least bit repentant. "Carriage rides are dull enough on pleasant days, but with nothing to look at for hours on end they're positively unbearable."

"It's one of the reasons I prefer travelling on horseback," Randolph said, the comment popping out of his mouth completely unbidden.

"If only I were able to do so," Lady Angelica said with a sigh. "Unfortunately, we ladies are only permitted to ride for sport. Mama would have a fit if I ever suggested going on a lengthy journey in such a way."

"An excellent reason for you to marry, my lady, since the right husband would not choose to hinder you thus." Where the devil were these words coming from? And when had he acquired such a flirtatious tone?

Lady Angelica tilted her head as if giving his comment serious consideration. "Do you think?" She glanced at Miss Harlow before returning her gaze to his. "In my experience, husbands tend to be more controlling than one's parents, not less."

"Then your experience must be limited to only intolerant men, for which I must extend apologies on behalf of my entire sex."

"Am I to understand that you would allow your wife to travel by horseback from, let us say, here to London?" An intensity burned in Lady Angelica's eyes, which he noted were not entirely brown but almost golden. She was testing him, he realized, judging his character and deciding whether she might consider him as a possible match.

Nothing thrilled him more.

"If it is her wish to do so and she has proven herself a capable horsewoman, then yes, I would, as long as she does not choose to ride alone."

Lady Angelica's mouth twitched slightly, as if deciding whether or not to smile. Randolph found himself holding his breath as he waited for her to give her opinion. Miss Harlow remained silent, which seemed to be her preferred state of being, so unless she showed a sudden interest in archaeology, his hobby of choice, he would have to dismiss her as a candidate.

But Lady Angelica...

"To do so would be remarkably foolish, my lord." And then, before he could fully appreciate what she'd said – the fact that she'd chosen to agree with him on a subject that seemed immensely important for some strange reason – she said, "By the way, I must commend you for handling Lady Seraphina as well as you did. A more polite man would have followed protocol."

"I—"

The supper bell rang and the doors to the dining room opened. Lady Angelica gave him a wry smile in parting as she went to find her mother, which was when Randolph noticed the ribbon trailing behind her. He shook his head in wonderment. Lady Angelica was unlike any woman he'd ever met before. She baffled him with her lack of finesse and the almost magnetic response he'd felt for her during their brief conversation. And what had she meant by her comment? That she considered him to be ill-mannered? It felt like she'd offered a compliment, but he rather feared she might not have.

Confused and oddly eager to spend more time in her company, Randolph entered the dining room with every hope that she'd been placed next to him. Instead, he found himself seated with Lady Seraphina and Miss St. James on either side and with Lady Angelica so far away at the opposite end of the table, she might as well have been sitting in China.

Randolph swallowed a groan and attempted a smile while he waited for all the ladies to be seated. Fleetingly, from behind a floral centerpiece, he caught Lady Angelica's eye. Humor danced there – laughter at his expense – but rather than feel offended or angered, his chest expanded with a warmth he'd not felt in years. Not since those long ago days before the world he knew had been torn apart at the seams.

Dulled by the memories, he struggled to return to the mood he'd been in only one second earlier. It turned out to be an impossible undertaking with Lady Seraphina listing all her exceptional qualities and Miss St. James looking like she'd rather be dead than forced to endure the company of others. But at least there was wine. Randolph managed a toast as a more formal way of welcoming everyone to his home, during which he deliberately avoided looking at Lady Angelica. He wasn't sure why, other than that it felt wrong to indulge in her sprightly charisma when his current frame of mind would only offer darkness in return.

Chapter Two

As the group assembled after dinner, Angelica wasn't sure what to make of Lord Sterling. He was certainly handsome with raven black hair falling slightly over his brow. His eyes were sharp – piercing – a sure sign of intelligence, his jawline square without being too angular, and his mouth, with its curving lower lip, so perfectly sculpted she could not stop looking at it. Strange thing, that.

But as pleasing as his looks might be, they would not last forever, which meant she was far more interested in his character. She liked that he'd chosen to meet her remarks head on with a bit of light banter. It spoke well of his sense of humor, for if there was one thing she could not stand the thought of, it was having to spend the rest of her life tied to a man who did not laugh.

And he'd even exhibited a pleasing amount of progressiveness with regard to the freedom he was willing to give his wife. Angelica liked that about him too. For although she knew her own father had treated her mother well, her brothers-in-law often chose to exert their authority over her sisters, preventing them from doing as they pleased.

Still, she'd noted a change of mood in Lord Sterling when they'd sat down to eat. It was almost as if his luster had faded.

Of course, it could simply be Lady Seraphina's doing. While Angelica was too far away to hear what the woman was saying, she could see her lips constantly moving to the point where even the saintliest person would likely be tempted to strangle her.

Now in the parlor, a small part of Angelica's heart hoped Lord Sterling might come to join her and Lucy. Instead, he chose to engage Miss Stevens in conversation at the opposite end of the room.

"He's the host," Lucy said as she reached for her teacup.

Angelica frowned. "I know."

"Then you also know that he must bestow his attention on all his viable options in equal measure."

It was difficult not to snort and sputter in response to such a comment. "You make it sound as though we're hats on a shelf at a milliner's shop and he's deciding to buy one."

Lucy sipped her tea, her expression thoughtful. "I like that analogy. It fits." Angelica sighed. She supposed her friend was right. "Not to worry. I'm sure he'll pick you in the end."

Angelica's head whipped round faster than a weathervane in a storm. "What?"

"He likes you."

"That's hardly enough," Angelica grumbled.

"It is when considering his selection," Lucy countered. "We're not any man's dream, Angelica. Hence the reason we're all still unwed. Although I don't understand why you would be, outgoing as you are."

"Outgoingness comes with a downside." She pursed her lips, took a quick sip of her tea, then set it aside. "I am forever blurting out things I ought to keep to myself. It's not the sort of quality most men seek when looking for a wife."

"In that case I have a feeling you may have found the first gentleman to be taken by such a trait." Lucy smiled. "Lord Sterling clearly enjoyed your comments on riding and on Lady Seraphina."

"Maybe, but that doesn't mean he'll pick me."

Lucy snorted. "Now you're either fishing for compliments or lying to yourself."

"Well, what about you?" Angelica asked. "He could choose you if you give him a chance to get to know you better."

"Perhaps," Lucy conceded.

"After all, there's little point in joining a competition unless you plan on doing your best to win it."

"I suppose that... Oh, here he comes."

Angelica forced herself to hide her excitement and not turn toward him too quickly. Her pulse had quickened, most likely due to the thrill of the game being played, for it couldn't possibly be on account of the man himself. Could it?

Of course not, she told herself. They'd barely met.

"I hope you'll pardon my intrusion," Lord Sterling said once he'd come to a halt in front of the sofa where Angelica and Lucy sat. "But I was rather hoping you might take a turn of the room with me, Lady Angelica."

"Oh...um..." And now she was stuttering like a fool. "I cannot possibly leave Miss Harlow alone."

"Of course you can," Lucy said. "I've no aversion to solitude. And if I should change my mind, I can always remove myself to another part of the room where conversation is more forthcoming."

"How sporting of you," Lord Sterling said with an obvious hint of admiration.

Angelica silently cheered on behalf of Lucy's perfectly delivered comment. "If you're sure..." She waited for Lucy to give a definitive nod before rising and placing her hand in the crook of Lord Sterling's arm. As they started forward, she mouthed a 'thank you' to her friend, who merely grinned and waved her off.

"Did you enjoy the meal?"

"I did, although I'm not especially fond of leek soup, veal, or flummery."

He frowned. "Was anything else served?"

"The vegetables were good, especially the potatoes."

A grin caught the edge of his mouth, softening his features. "What would you have preferred?"

Angelica smiled. She appreciated his question and his lack of annoyance with her since most hosts would have been appalled by her criticism. "To start, a smoked filet of trout served with dill and lemon. Next, oven roasted duck stuffed with apples and prunes, accompanied by sugar glazed potatoes and sautéed red cabbage. And lastly...a lemon syllabub, I should think."

"I would not have thought it possible, but I'm actually getting hungry again." The warmth in Lord Sterling's eyes as he said this was unmistakable. "It is certainly a menu worth trying one day."

Good heavens. What was wrong with her stomach? It felt as though it was spinning around like an out of control top. Angelica sucked in a breath. Her cheeks felt warm and her legs seemed to struggle with keeping her upright.

"Tell me something," Lord Sterling said once they'd passed the spot where the mothers and chaperones had chosen to gather. "How do you find Colchester Hall?"

"It's impressive. But I'm not sure I'd want to live here."

Lord Sterling jerked on her arm. Did he trip over something?

"I beg your pardon?" For the first time since she'd met him, he sounded affronted.

Ah well. Angelica supposed his tolerance of her until this point was bound to meet with an end sooner or later. "It's not a home."

"It's *my* home," he snapped, then catching himself, gently added, "it will also be the home of the future Lady Sterling."

"You mistake my meaning," Angelica told him because really, why stop now? "It's too big and vast, too cold and drafty, completely devoid of cozy homeliness."

Oh dear. He was now staring at her as if her hair had suddenly decided to turn a bright shade of blue. "Cozy homeliness?"

"Take this room for example. It's got to be ten times the size of any other parlor I've ever seen."

"Space is important. I always find small rooms too cramped."

"Certainly," she agreed, acknowledging his point with a dip of her head. "But look at how far apart all the pieces of furniture have been placed. If you choose to sit in that sofa over there, you cannot possibly carry on a conversation with the person opposite without shouting."

"Naturally, I would converse with the person sitting beside me," he said as if she were the most thickheaded woman he'd ever encountered.

Angelica bristled. "It isn't practical, nor does it offer the sort of welcoming atmosphere I would be drawn to. You'd be much better off moving that sofa over there and then adding one more seating arrangement over here. A gaming table would work well too as an alternative, and..."

"And what?" he asked her tightly.

She swallowed, unsure if it was wise of her to continue. Then again, she had come this far so why on earth not? "Rugs. Preferably in burgundy tones to complement the pale green upholstery."

"Right." They'd arrived back at the spot where they'd started. He released her arm, took a step back. "You've given me a great deal to think about, my lady. I do hope you enjoy the rest of your evening." Upon which he strode away, directly toward the door leading out to the hallway.

Mrs. Essex stood there and Lord Sterling soon joined her. They exchanged a few words and then, with one swift backward glance and no parting words to his guests, he left the parlor with her. But what struck Angelica as particularly odd was the look in Mrs. Essex's eyes when she'd met Angelica's gaze. It was almost as if she'd been laughing at her.

"How was it?" Lucy asked.

Angelica shook off the uneasy feeling the housekeeper gave her and turned to her friend. "I fear I ruined my chances." She returned to the seat she'd vacated earlier.

"Surely it can't have been that bad." Lucy was carefully nibbling on a small chocolate-covered biscuit.

"Well," Angelica told her with a sigh, "I told him I disliked the food and found his home lacking. Frankly, it's a wonder he didn't insult me in return."

"Hmm... There's always a chance he likes honest women."

"I was blunt to the point of rudeness, Lucy. And I don't even know why, but it couldn't be helped. Once I started talking there was no stopping the words. It was awful."

"Perhaps another cup of tea would make you feel better?"

"Thank you, but I think I'd prefer to retire for the evening. I'll just inform my mother."

"I'll come upstairs with you." Lucy brushed the crumbs from her fingers and stood. "No sense in me staying here without you or my host."

Ten minutes later, after pointing out to her mother that Lord Sterling had abandoned them all in favor of lord knew what, Angelica said good night to Lucy outside her bedchamber door and went to prepare for bed. The same maid who'd unpacked her things earlier responded when she rang the bell pull. She didn't say much while she worked, which was fine with Angelica since enough things had happened today to occupy her brain without her having to engage in small talk with a servant.

"Will that be all?" the maid, whose name turned out to be Emma, asked once she'd finished combing Angelica's hair.

"Yes. Thank you."

"Then I'll wish you a pleasant night, my lady." Emma bobbed a quick curtsey and departed, shutting the door behind her.

Angelica stared at it for a moment, then glanced toward the door connecting her room with her mother's. She was tempted to open it, but resisted the urge. It was just that the feeling she'd had in here earlier – of cold fingers creeping over her skin – was back.

She shook her head and laughed at her silliness, then glanced at her book which lay waiting for her on the bedside table. Clearly she'd become too engrossed in her English translation of *Fantasmagoriana* if elements were becoming part of her own reality.

Still... She bit her lip, then grinned as she climbed into bed and picked up the novel. She simply *had* to know what happened next. Settling back against her pillows, Angelica opened it and started to read. She liked how the book was compiled of short stories that were reasonably quick to get through. Right now, she was in the middle of "The Death Bride," right at the point where Marino had gone in pursuit of a masked woman.

Angelica turned the page. The woman seemed to have disappeared into thin air. Intrigued, Angelica kept reading until she reached the spot where Marino's fiancée, Ida, returned to the ball in search of him, only to be told he'd just left with her. Good heavens, how was that possible? Unless...

The flame from Angelica's oil lamp flickered, distorting the golden light. A melodious chime from the clock on the fireplace mantle announced the hour. Angelica flexed her toes. Her feet felt like ice, and the feeling seemed to be travelling slowly up her legs. She pulled the blankets more firmly around her entire body, cocooning herself.

The flame from her oil lamp flickered again, then guttered as if struggling to stay lit.

"No, no, no," Angelica muttered. She had to finish the story. She had to know what had happened to Marino and how there could possibly be two Idas.

Ignoring the chill which had now seeped into her fingers, she strained her eyes to see the black print. Until the flame gave one last burst of light and died.

The room transformed into a collection of gray and dark purple tones. With a sigh of frustration, Angelica climbed from her bed and hugged her arms around her body. Padding across the floor, she approached the connecting door, intending to listen for her mother's presence. If she was still up, Angelica could simply read the rest of the story in her room.

But as she passed the window, a breeze swept over her ankles.

Angelica turned to see the curtains move ever so gently, perhaps on account of a draft? She decided to check by carefully pulling the fabric aside and running her fingers along the edge of the window. Nothing. Only darkness. The glass itself was streaked by water, distorting her reflection.

A prickly sensation spread like a rash across the nape of her neck.

Something moved in the window's reflection – a shadow behind her.

She instinctively turned.

Her breath filled the air like smoke and her fingers grew rigid like twigs. Swallowing hard, Angelica stared at her bedchamber door, certain she'd locked it. Yet now it stood open.

She blinked. Someone had been in her room while she'd been standing here lost in thought. Mrs. Essex perhaps, or the viscount himself? Angelica crossed the floor in search of an answer and reached the hallway just in time to glimpse the fluttering hem of nightgown as it disappeared round a corner.

Barefoot, she ran toward it, desperate to chase down the person and give them a piece of her mind. But when she reached the stairs, there was nothing. Heart pounding and with her bones aching from cold, she glanced down into the foyer.

A shadow crept slowly across the wall.

How had the individual managed to descend the stairs so quickly?

Determined to catch the elusive person, Angelica balled her frozen hands into fists and quickened her pace. If only she'd thought to put on her robe and slippers to ward off the ever-increasing frigidity.

By the time she reached the foyer, she was trembling from head to toe.

She glanced around. The chill had dug its claws into her chest. She struggled for breath. A movement, right at the edge of her vision, caused her to turn.

A hallway was there.

Angelica started forward. "Wait," she called out, even though the person was clearly intent on escape. A whisper of air fluttered over her shoulders. She glanced back, certain she'd see someone there, but all she found was empty darkness.

"It's all right," she whispered to herself. "Nothing to be afraid of." Yet there was a feeling, right in the middle of her heart, that told her something wasn't quite right.

Ignoring it, Angelica kept going, following the shadow through twists and turns until she arrived at a tall wooden door.

She blinked.

The space was empty.

She glanced around, searching for someone who'd hidden in the darkness. Nothing caught her attention. Not one single movement. And then she heard it – a hoarse cry for help, so thin and desperate it curdled her blood. She stared at the door. The sound was coming from the opposite side, accompanied by...

Angelica's heart thumped.

It sounded like scratching.

With a shudder, she took a step forward.

Someone was there. Someone who needed her help.

She reached for the bolt with frozen fingers and unlocked the door. It flew open, yanked from her grasp on a blast of cold air as wind and rain whipped her face. Angelica searched the darkness, but no one was there. And yet she knew she'd seen something...heard a distinct voice crying for help.

It made no sense.

Unless she'd imagined it all.

Maybe she'd failed to close her bedchamber door properly. She blinked, still staring through the rain, unable to understand. In the distance, she glimpsed the outline of the pavilion she could see from her bedchamber window.

Her heart lurched as she recalled Mrs. Essex's words from earlier.

"What the devil do you think you're doing?"

Angelica spun around with a jolt. Lord Sterling's glare was harder than granite as he yanked her away from the door and shut it.

He crossed his arms and leaned forward just enough to meet her gaze at eye level. "Why are you here?"

"I, um..." It was difficult to gather her wits when he looked at her with such menace.

"Yes?" He took a step forward, forcing her back, until she met the uneven stone wall behind her.

"I thought I saw someone come this way."

"Nobody comes this way," he told her harshly. "Not anymore."

"I—" He grabbed her unceremoniously by the arm and proceeded to escort her back the way she'd come. "My lord. Please. You're hurting me."

"Did Mrs. Essex not tell you specifically not to venture into this part of the house?" He practically dragged her up the stairs, heedless of her plea for him to loosen his grip.

"I—"

"You are forbidden from opening that door. Is that clear?"

Her toes caught the top step, causing her to stumble. "Yes. Yes, I promise." She didn't understand his reasoning much less the rest of this night's events, but she would adhere to his wishes. It was the least she could do as his guest.

"And for God's sake," he added as he deposited her outside her bedchamber door a while later, "put on a robe and some slippers if you really must leave your room at night. Otherwise, you risk catching a chill."

"Of course. I didn't think."

"Clearly not." The rugged planes of his face were emphasized in the darkness. His mouth was just a harsh line. "Good night, my lady."

"Good night." Angelica wasn't sure if he heard her since he was already walking away.

Unable to make sense of what had transpired, Angelica climbed back into her bed. Her mind was a muddle. It all seemed so real but how could that possibly be? She snuggled deeper under the blankets and yawned. Tomorrow she'd look for some answers, because one thing was certain: there simply had to be a logical explanation.

RANDOLPH BURST INTO his bedchamber with such violence he almost managed to unhinge the door. Struggling for breath, he crossed the floor and poured a large measure of brandy, downed it, and poured himself another. God help him, it had been two years! Two bloody years and all it took for rage and guilt to grip him once more was seeing Lady Angelica standing in that cursed doorway.

He'd thought he was past this. He'd thought he'd managed to put Katrina to rest. Yet here she was, haunting him from beyond the grave by reminding him of the fool he'd once been and of how he'd failed to save her.

Christ!

His fingers tightened around the glass. Blood rushed through his veins. A sharp stabbing pain ripped through his skull. The glass shattered with a dissatisfying crunch that brought a sting to the palm of his hand.

Damn.

Randolph reached inside his jacket pocket and pulled out a handkerchief. The white piece of linen was soon covered in blotches of red. He sighed and lowered himself to the armchair that stood before the fire. He'd removed himself to this part of the building after Katrina's death, because he couldn't stand being anywhere near the spot where she'd perished, her cries for help blocked out by the howling wind.

His chest rose with uneasy movements. And now there was Lady Angelica. As his heartbeats settled into a steadier rhythm and the anger roiling inside him abated, he recalled how she'd looked when he'd found her. His body tensed in response to what his brain was only now letting him realize. She'd been delectable, clad in only her nightgown, the fabric so fine it revealed her shapely curves and the hem so short he'd caught a glimpse of her ankles.

Perhaps if she'd not been in a state of confusion and he'd not gotten so angry, he could have used the situation to his advantage. He could have kissed her, if she'd let him.

Would she have?

He wasn't entirely sure.

Her criticism of Colchester Hall made him wonder if she'd ever want to accept an offer of marriage from him. Of course, the biggest problem was she was now the only woman who interested him remotely. Her bluntness intrigued him. It superseded her perplexing desire to explore his home at night, wandering into places that didn't concern her. Especially since he had a feeling she would respect his wishes from now on. But personality and character, those were things that couldn't be changed, and although it had only been one day – or really just one evening – he could not deny the pleasure he'd found in her company.

She'd been more than just blunt, he acknowledge with a slow smile. She'd been fun and entertaining – a breath of fresh air he so desperately needed.

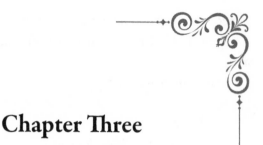

Chapter Three

Angelica stared out of her bedchamber window the following morning at the spot directly below, where Lord Sterling's wife had allegedly perished. She touched her fingertips to the windowpane, pressing gently against the glass while wondering how such a thing could have happened.

When she'd woken, roughly half an hour earlier, her first instinct had been to dismiss last night's occurrence as a dream. Or a nightmare. Perhaps Lord Sterling had found her walking in her sleep. According to her mother, she'd done so as a child. She nodded. That had to be it. She must have fallen asleep reading "The Death Bride," only to dream up a ghost story of her own.

Considering Colchester Hall's history, it wasn't so odd. In fact, the manor served as the perfect backdrop for any terrifying tale. Satisfied with this explanation, Angelica blew out a breath and allowed herself to relax. She'd head downstairs for breakfast, and if she found Lucy there, she'd invite her for a walk now that the rain had stopped.

Throwing a shawl over her shoulders, Angelica left her room and started toward the stairs. She hadn't gone more than three paces, though, before she was forced to stop and glance over her shoulder. No one was there, yet it felt as though someone were watching her every move. A shiver raced down her spine and her heart beat faster, sensing what she couldn't see.

Some...*thing* was there.

No.

No. No. No.

It wasn't possible. It wasn't real.

She quickened her pace until she was almost running. The stairs were right there, she just had to reach them. She just...had to round this last corner.

"Heavens! Is everything all right, my lady?"

Mrs. Essex suddenly stood before her, studying her with keen curiosity.

"I'm sorry," Angelica gasped. She'd nearly barreled straight into the woman. It had taken supreme force of will to reverse her direction. But at least the dreadful sensation creeping up behind her had finally vanished.

Mrs. Essex frowned and tried to look past her. "Was someone chasing you?"

Angelica stared back, then blinked. "No." But she wasn't entirely sure. She'd felt something awful. Something not of this world. Or perhaps it was once again her overactive imagination playing tricks on her mind. She wasn't sure what to believe anymore.

Mrs. Essex smiled with an almost irritating degree of pleasantness. "Why don't you go downstairs and enjoy a good breakfast. I'm sure you'll feel better after a hot cup of tea."

"Yes. Thank you."

Mrs. Essex's smile widened as she stepped aside so Angelica could pass. There was something about this woman –

something distinctly unsettling. Angelica's stomach clenched as she walked away from her, not on account of fear this time but because of another feeling she couldn't quite place. It only worsened when, upon reaching the foyer, she looked up to find Mrs. Essex still there. The woman watched her with that pleasant smile of hers, though there was now a pensiveness to her expression.

Shuddering, Angelica made her way to the dining room where breakfast was already underway. It seemed she was the last to arrive. "Good morning," she said, deliberately keeping her gaze from Lord Sterling as she went to fill a plate for herself at the side table.

"I'm sorry I came down without you," Rose said. She'd brought her plate over for a refill of bacon, for which she harbored a particular fondness. "But I thought it best to let you rest."

"It's quite all right, Mama," Angelica assured her while wondering whether to try the strawberry jam or the peach preserves. "How did you sleep?"

"Very well. I went up shortly after you and fell asleep almost instantly. How about you?"

"Fine." Angelica spooned some peach preserves onto her plate.

"Are you sure?" Rose was definitely frowning based on the tone of her voice. "You don't sound like your usual cheery self."

"I had a bad dream. That's all. Nothing a hearty breakfast and a cup of hot tea can't fix."

"Not to mention the attentions of our handsome host. Don't think I didn't notice you were the only lady with whom he took a turn of the parlor last night."

"That doesn't mean anything," Angelica whispered.

Rose tilted her head and gave her a *don't-be-silly* look. "It means he singled you out."

"Perhaps," Angelica allowed. But she was fairly certain she'd bungled whatever chance she'd had of him choosing her. First, by offending him and second, by enraging him to the point where he'd appeared ready to do serious violence. "But what if I don't want him?"

Her mother blanched. "Don't even jest about such a thing. We need this match, Angelica. *You* need it." Rose's lips quivered ever so slightly at the corners. "I didn't want to worry you but my funds are limited. Bloomfield has not been as generous as I'd have hoped, and as a result, I may lose the house."

Angelica's mouth dropped open. "What?"

"The many expenses left me no choice but to borrow against it."

"You never said a word." The modest townhouse with its prestigious address on Berkley Square had been purchased by Angelica's father when her oldest sister, Stephanie, was born. The purpose had been to create a cozier family home than the grand Bloomfield House manor on the edge of Hyde Park would allow. In his will, Angelica's father had bequeathed the property to his wife. It was Angelica's childhood home – the house in which she'd always lived – and the thought of losing it because her father's cousin was being tight fisted made her feel ill.

"Come. Let us sit down before we attract too much attention."

Angelica couldn't move. Her mother had just dropped a cannonball on her head, yet she wanted to sit down and eat as if all was normal? "We need to discuss this, Mama. Surely my sisters can help?"

"They already have."

And she refused to ask them for further assistance? "But even if I marry well, there's no guarantee my husband will—"

"No," Rose said. She looked somewhat piqued. "I would never expect him to, nor would I want to be anyone's burden. What I am saying is that I may have to relocate to something significantly smaller."

Understanding dawned. Her mother feared her financial straits would force her to move to a place where there wouldn't be room for her unmarried daughter. Angelica instinctively glanced toward Lord Sterling, who made no effort to hide the fact that he was watching her with keen interest. Her heart quickened a little and she tightened her grip on her plate. How could she possibly marry a man who was capable of such forceful anger?

"Come," her mother insisted once more, and this time she walked away, returning to the table without waiting for Angelica to follow.

Angelica dropped her gaze to her plate. All she wanted was to toss it against the wall in despair, but that would be wasteful, not to mention ill-bred, and she actually was quite hungry. So she clenched her jaw and went to sit beside Miss Chesterfield since all the other seats were already taken. It was just as well. Lucy would only want to talk and right now that was the last thing Angelica felt like doing.

Instead, she ate while pondering what her mother had told her.

HAVING FINISHED HIS food a while ago, Randolph enjoyed his morning coffee. He tried to engage the women seated closest to him in conversation, though not without keeping a constant eye on Lady Angelica. Her face had been drawn when she'd entered the room. Now, after speaking with her mother, concern strained her features. And she was making a very deliberate effort to keep from looking at him. Really, he had to apologize for his behavior last night. After all, his intention was to woo her, not frighten her away.

"Perhaps you would like to know the schedule for the coming week?" He wasn't foolish enough to invite six young ladies to his home with no plan to entertain them. All directed their gazes at him, chaperones included. Except Lady Angelica, whose attention remained fixed on the contents of her teacup. "Today I'll be spending a private hour with each of you so we can improve our acquaintance."

In a way he dreaded it, for he knew at least two of the candidates would have little to say. At least not enough to fill a whole hour. He also wasn't sure there was much point to the effort when only Lady Angelica held his interest. Still, they'd all come a long way for his consideration and deserved to be given a chance.

"The rain has ceased and if the weather stays dry we shall go for a walk tomorrow. If it's not too cold, we can even enjoy a picnic. Then on Wednesday, we shall go to the village. There's a lovely little teashop and a haberdashery where you may find ribbons and lace to your hearts' content. Friday is set aside for games, including a treasure hunt Mrs. Essex has promised she'll arrange." This was met with particular murmurs of excitement and even a quick glance from Lady Angelica. Randolph smiled. "On Saturday, I shall host a ball – the neighboring gentry have already been invited. And on Sunday I shall ask one of you to stay on an extra week, at the end of which I will propose."

There were several pink cheeks after this declaration and even a few low chuckles and self-conscious smiles. Randolph's only interest was in Lady Angelica's response. She neither smiled nor blushed but rather bit her lip and frowned harder. And then she looked at him, her gaze locking with his in a hard stare comprised of sheer determination.

His chest tightened and his heart – that part of him that scarcely knew how to function any more – slumped. It was the only way he could think of describing the overwhelming disappointed that filled him. Because he wanted...he wanted...

Oh, hell.

He wanted her to truly want him, not just because of his title or because she needed to marry, but because thinking of him as her husband felt right – because she was drawn to him. God, they scarcely knew each other, had only just met the previous day. It was absurd of him to have such a yearning, yet it couldn't be helped. He wanted more from Lady Angelica than from the rest.

Idiot.

Tightening his jaw, he addressed Lady Seraphina. "Would you be kind enough to meet me in the green parlor in half an hour?"

"I'd be delighted." She practically glowed with the pleasure of being the first he'd selected to join him. Little did she know that he'd merely done it in order to get her out of the way as quickly as possible.

With nothing left to say, Randolph stood, excused himself, and left the dining room. Six hours later, with only an hour's reprieve during luncheon, he was almost ready to hang himself from the rafters in the attic. Lady Seraphina had shown no interest in him at all, except when it came to inquiring about his properties, the number of carriages he owned, and how much time he spent in London. Everything else she said pertained either to herself, her father's magnificent title, or her family's close connection to the king.

And then there were Miss Stevens, Miss Chesterfield, and Miss St. James who all seemed to blend into one big mass of blandness. It had been a chore getting any of them to say much of anything. Miss St. James had been especially withdrawn. She had not opened up as her chaperone had assured him she would. Instead, she'd kept her gaze averted from his while offering nods and headshakes by way of response. If he asked a question that demanded more, she'd wait an unbearable ten seconds before mumbling something he couldn't understand.

So it had been a delightful surprise when Miss Harlow, though somewhat soft spoken and timid, had made a couple of jokes and proven herself to be more than he'd expected. She even answered every question he'd prepared to perfection, proving herself to be, on paper at least, an excellent choice.

"Thank you for an entertaining discussion," he told her once their time was up. "It has been most enlightening."

She smiled prettily. Really, there was something beguiling about her he'd not noticed before – perhaps in her eyes or the curve of her mouth? Not that she compared with Lady

Angelica, whose looks, though not stunning by any means, captivated him in an entirely different way. Plain and simple, he found her to be incredibly attractive, not just physically, but...

Well, it was her personality really.

"Likewise," Miss Harlow told him. She seemed to consider the partially open door leading out to the hallway. There was a sense of hesitance about her – an indecision of sorts – until she suddenly met his gaze with a forthrightness he would not have thought her capable of. "Most men would have chosen an entirely different group of candidates." She didn't sound accusatory, just as if she were making a clear observation.

Randolph couldn't disagree. He certainly wasn't about to argue her point since that would most likely insult her intelligence. So he chose to say nothing as they stood across from each other in silence. It wasn't uncomfortable, though he did feel as if she were taking his measure.

"Shall I send Lady Angelica in?" she eventually asked. "I believe she is the last to enjoy the pleasure of your company."

He almost laughed, because he was almost certain Lady Angelica wouldn't consider it a pleasure, though he definitely meant to convince her otherwise. "Please do."

Miss Harlow gave a small nod. She moved as if to exit the room, and he almost turned away to prepare himself for Lady Angelica's arrival. But Miss Harlow suddenly stopped. It seemed she had one more thing to say. "It is often helpful to be faced with undesirable options, for it tends to make the obvious choice so much clearer."

She was gone before he was able to respond. Her insight had literally stripped him of words, for it was quite unexpected, not only because it had come from a woman who, while proving to be a better conversationalist than Miss St. James, was still a hesitant speaker, but because he was sure the choice she referred to was someone besides herself.

Randolph blinked. Miss Harlow might not be for him, but she was certainly a woman he could respect and admire. And then all thought of her vanished from his mind as Lady Angelica entered the room. Her hands were clasped before her, and she appeared apprehensive in a way that unnerved him. He didn't want her to feel uncomfortable in his presence or for her to look so unlike the smiling woman with whom he'd conversed last night. He wanted her as blunt as she had been then, for it had occurred to him that while she'd managed to ruffle his feathers, only someone truly honest would speak as candidly as she had done, and this was something he truly valued.

"Would you care for some tea while we talk?" He gestured toward the sofa, hoping she'd choose it in favor of the armchair so he might sit beside her.

She glanced over her shoulder and shivered. Not a good sign.

But then she gave a small nod. "Tea would be nice."

A RUSTLING SOUND WHISPERED close to Angelica's ear, causing her to glance back as she'd done on countless occasions that morning. Of course nothing was there. She knew before she looked, yet she still couldn't shake the feeling she was being watched from a corner – just off to one side where her gaze didn't reach. Shivering, she accepted Lord

Sterling's offer of tea. Anything to take her mind off the strange sensations following her wherever she went in this house.

Lord Sterling rang for a maid, who brought a fresh pot and cups to replace the ones he and Lucy had used. Angelica took a deep breath and approached the seating arrangement, electing to sit in the armchair. Lord Sterling appeared to ponder her choice for a moment, then lowered himself to the spot on the sofa closest to her.

"I realize you must have had enough tea today to last you a lifetime," she said since she was the only woman present and therefor ought to pour, "but would you care for another?"

When he didn't respond, she glanced at him more directly than she had all day. His mouth tilted, the edge of his lips drawing up to form a crooked sort of smile. "I would love one," he murmured, just low enough for his voice to create a vibration within her. "Thank you."

Angelica swallowed. Was her heart truly fluttering now and why oh why did she have to look at him when all that did was muddle her head? This was the last reaction she wanted toward a man who'd yelled at her in anger and given her arm a dark bruise.

Dropping her gaze to the teapot, she took a calming breath and filled both cups. "You don't seem like the milk or sugar sort. Correct?"

"Indeed." He raised an eyebrow. She wasn't sure how she knew this without looking at him, but she did, perhaps because of his tone. "An impressive deduction."

The air shifted around her shoulders – there was that rustling noise once more. Angelica forced herself to stay still, to not look over her shoulder, for she knew she'd find nothing there. So she reached for her cup and cradled it between her hands. It would still be too hot to drink, but the warmth offered comfort.

"I, um..." Lord Sterling cleared his throat. A pause followed. Angelica reluctantly looked up. "I wish to apologize to you for last night."

It wasn't the color of his eyes that spoke to her, but the earnest need for understanding and forgiveness they conveyed. "It was wrong of me to thwart your wishes."

"Nevertheless, I should have been kinder. More gentle." The edges of his mouth tightened as if with discomfort. "It is not in my nature to hurt women. I'm not that sort of man."

"I know." She couldn't explain how she knew this, but she did. "You were upset, not so much by my presence but, I imagine, by what I reminded you of."

He closed his eyes. "Yes." Barely a whisper, but enough to confirm what she'd started suspecting.

"Will you tell me about your wife?"

"Will *you* tell *me* what your mother said to you at breakfast this morning?" he countered.

She pressed her lips together and frowned. "I do not wish to marry you."

There she went again, speaking her mind with no care for who she stampeded in the process. He opened his mouth as if to comment. Instead, he just sat there, staring at her as if she were the strangest creature he'd ever seen.

"In truth, I've no desire to marry anyone," she felt compelled to add. The additional discussions she'd had with her mother after breakfast had, however, forced Angelica to view her situation with increased clarity. And since she didn't want to be selfish or cause her mother additional worry, she hadn't much choice.

"But," she told him carefully, "the time has come for me to forget my own wants and do my duty instead. I'm sure it's not what you're hoping to hear but I am a practical woman. I cannot pretend I've been swept off my feet unless that is how I actually feel."

"Good."

It was her turn to stare at him. "Good?"

"I don't care for pretense. Honesty and straightforwardness are far more desirable."

She gave him a slow nod. "Then I should also tell you that I'll expect my husband to help support my mother. She could lose her London home and I...I just cannot bear to—"

"Angelica." His voice was warm, but firm. Reassuring. "You mustn't concern yourself about that. If we marry, I will guarantee your mother's wellbeing."

"You would pay for her house?"

"As long as you never betray me, I will do all I can to keep you happy." He stood, quite suddenly and offered her his hand. "Will you accompany me over there to that window?"

She thought of saying no, then realized she wanted to go with him.

So she placed her hand in his and immediately sucked in a breath as a shock of awareness surged up her arm.

"Come," he urged, as if nothing untoward had happened.

She stood and together they crossed the floor, though not without her being acutely aware of his warmth, the enticing scent of bergamot that clung to his clothes and just...him.

Angelica's pulse quickened.

"I believe it is my turn to be honest with you." Lord Sterling still held her hand yet she felt no compulsion to pull away. Indeed, she liked feeling the warmth of his skin against hers. There was a rightness to it that defied explanation. "Ordinarily, I would refuse to speak of Katrina. In fact, I have not uttered her name since the day she died. But there's a genuine quality to you that tells me you'll never be my wife unless I tell you exactly what happened."

It was curious, Angelica decided. For two people who'd only just met, they understood each other remarkably well. And yet... "You're mistaken. I will marry you no matter what. For my mother's sake."

He tilted his head. "I do not doubt it. But marrying me and actually being my wife are two very separate things." His eyes burned with hot intensity until she felt herself scorched. He was speaking of intimacies. The sort that forged unbreakable bonds – the kind that demanded trust.

"I see."

"I hardly think so." He chuckled, deep in his throat. "But you will. As long as you never betray me."

The skin at the back of Angelica's neck prickled. Lord Sterling's eyes had darkened, hardened as if by an unpleasant memory. Unease slithered through her, and the air around her grew cooler. A strange sense of panic started building inside her – a sudden fear of knowing too much.

But then he spoke, and it was too late for her to change her mind, to press her hand to his mouth and force him into silence, to remain oblivious.

"I loved her." He said it as if there had been no choice. Angelica's heart paused to absorb this before continuing its steady rhythm. "She was perfect and we were happy together. Happier than I ever expected to be. Until she died, frozen to death outside and..." The muscles in his throat flexed and strained as if he were struggling to speak.

"I'm so sorry." Angelica waited for him to continue. When he didn't, she said, "Surely she must have called for help."

"There was a storm that night. No one would have heard her above the howling of the wind."

Angelica shuddered. The image Lord Sterling evoked of his wife's passing was thoroughly disturbing, especially in light of her own recent experiences. She swallowed. "It was the door from last night, wasn't it? The one that shut her out in the cold?"

His expression was pulled into grim lines, his eyes a dull shade of grey. "Again, I must apologize for my reaction."

"There's really no need."

He blinked, seemed to collect himself. His eyes focused on her with remarkable clarity. The air between them thickened. Her breaths came slower, harder. She parted her lips without even thinking. And then the air between them was gone, and his mouth was pressed against hers with insatiable hunger.

Surprise made her flinch and for a brief second he paused. Yes or no, he seemed to ask.

"What if someone sees?"

"No one will." His breath whispered softly against her lips. "They'd have to enter the room completely to see this corner. And the door isn't fully open."

Still, she hesitated, though only for a brief second before his scent and the desperate desire to ease away his sorrow in some small way overwhelmed her. She wanted this. She wanted him. And he must have felt her compliance, for he closed the gap between them once more with a kiss that reached to the depth of her soul.

This was passion and desire – it had to be – and she was alive with it, so alive every nerve ending in her body clamored for more. Her lips parted instinctively, and he wasted no time in taking advantage. Good lord! Whoever knew it would feel so grand to be devoured? His hand slid down her back, its progress slow, assessing, gauging her willingness and her reaction.

Angelica gasped. Not because she objected to his caress, but because of the air brushing over the nape of her neck. Ice dug its way under her skin like claws trying to rake their way through her. "I..." She drew back. "Do you feel that?"

His eyebrows drew together in bewilderment. "What?"

She glanced about. The chill trickled down her spine, slowly releasing its grip. "I'm referring to the cold."

He stared at her. "We are near the window. Perhaps you're more sensitive to the lower temperature in this part of the room than I am."

"Of course." That had to be it, right? Any other explanation would border on madness. She shivered. "Perhaps I should make a habit of wearing a shawl while I'm here."

"Perhaps," he agreed.

His gaze drove into hers in a way that made her heart pound with longing. Something warm touched her hand, almost causing her to leap. She relaxed when she realized it was his fingers, slowly sliding over her skin in a way that pushed all else to the background. She forgot her unease and relaxed once more while allowing herself to savor his touch.

"I want you to know..." His mouth flattened in a serious manner. He swallowed in an almost awkward sort of way. "I haven't kissed any of the others. Only you."

It felt important. Monumentally so. Yet she still had to ask, "Why?"

"Because I don't want them. I want you."

Angelica's lips parted in surprise. She hadn't expected him to be quite to frank. "You barely know me."

"I know you're the only woman here with whom I can see myself spending the rest of my life. Whether or not it will come to that will be determined in the coming days."

"You already know I don't care for Colchester Hall. What if I don't want to live here?"

The edges around his mouth tightened and he released her hand. Stepping away from her, he watched her through narrowed eyes. "This is my ancestral home. I cannot rid myself of it simply because you wish it."

"No. Of course you—"

"But" –he held up a hand— "I could perhaps be persuaded to spend more time in London."

"Really?" He merely inclined his head by way of answer. Angelica bit her lip and considered the sacrifice he was ready to make. "Thank you. For everything you're offering to do."

He shrugged one shoulder and strolled toward the side table. She followed and watched as he poured two glasses of port, their still-full teacups on the table completely forgotten. "We're merely trying to learn if an understanding can be reached." He held one glass toward her, and she stepped forward to take it. "Marriage requires compromise. Don't think I won't ask for anything in return."

Angelica gazed up at him. There was something mesmerizing in the way he looked at her. "Like what?" She had to know.

"I won't endure another marriage in which my wife and I sleep apart."

Her face heated. "Really?" The word was more of a squeak than something one might consider part of the English language.

His lips curved into the most devilish smile she'd ever seen. "I have needs, Angelica. And I will expect you to tend to them."

Good lord, the way he said her name, like a sensual purr. And the words themselves, what they implied... It was scandalous in the extreme – *he* was being scandalous and... and a secret part of her deep down inside thrilled at it.

"I see I have shocked you," he murmured. A low chuckle followed. "Sip your drink. It will help you regain your balance."

She did as he suggested. "I am usually the one to shock others with my boldness."

"How does it feel, having the favor returned?"

The answer crossed her lips without any thought. "Reassuring." It was baffling, but it was the truth. "It is comforting to know what one can expect."

"Precisely the reason why I am so partial to you."

Unsure of what else to say, Angelica glanced at the door and...glanced at it again. A dark shadow was there, just beyond the light, and the chill that had gripped her earlier hooked its claws into her shoulders.

She gasped. "I think someone's watching."

"Where?"

She looked back at him and pointed. "Right there."

"I don't see anyone." He crossed to the door and opened it wide, but before he reached it Angelica saw that the shadow was gone. "It was probably just a servant or one of the other guests passing by."

"Yes," she whispered, because to suggest anything else would only urge him to cart her off to Bedlam instead of to the altar. "You're probably right." She forced a smile and set her glass aside. Perhaps she was merely tired and it had been a trick of the light. "It is getting late. I should go upstairs if I am to get ready in time for dinner."

"By all means." He placed his glass on the fireplace mantle and reached for her hand. "It has been a true pleasure." Holding her gaze, he raised her hand to his lips.

Her stomach did a funny flip, and her skin turned all jittery. "Likewise," she managed, thankfully getting the word out without it sounding too strangled. Taking a deep breath, she turned and made her way to the door on slightly wobbly legs.

"Angelica?" He halted her right before she managed to slip out of the room.

Her heart knocked against her ribs as she glanced over her shoulder. "Yes?"

Dark eyes met hers. "How did you like the kiss?"

She considered something proper like, "it was pleasant" or, "very much." But she knew he liked her for her boldness and her unvarnished honesty, and if there was ever a time for both, this was it.

So she drew back her shoulders, met his gaze dead on, and smiled. "It was spectacular, my lord."

"Randolph." There was something hot and needy in the way he said it. "I want you to call me Randolph."

"Very well." Her fingers curled around the edge of the door, latching on in an effort to hold herself steady. And then she tested the name. "Randolph." His eyes lit up, egging her on. "I hope we have a chance to do it again."

"That can certainly be arranged."

And because she sensed he was on the verge of stalking toward her, shutting the door, and ravaging her right there where she stood, she departed before he had the chance to do something quite so damning.

Chapter Four

Dinner that evening was a wonderful affair. Angelica could scarcely believe her eyes when she received her first plate, filled with smoked trout, neatly arranged on a bed of lettuce with dill and a twisted slice of lemon on top. She stared at the dish, then glanced toward Lord Sterling. *Randolph.* He listened to Lady Seraphina – or at least pretended to, for his eyes clearly rested on Angelica and the secretive smile brushing his lips was directed at her.

"How wonderful," Rose remarked. "I love smoked trout and I dare say it's one of your favorite dishes as well, Angelica."

"It certainly is," Angelica said. Her cheeks burned, but that didn't stop her from returning Randolph's smile. Efforts like this, she decided, had to be rewarded, no matter what.

And not just the trout was perfect. Next came oven roasted duck, accompanied by baked apples and prunes, sugar glazed potatoes and sautéed red cabbage. Angelica kept her gaze fixed on her plate this time, for she feared all the other guests would somehow see the truth in her expression the moment she looked up. Randolph was openly favoring her – courting her with grand gestures in front of the other young ladies hoping to win his attention.

It felt underhanded somehow and yet...

Good lord, the food tasted good!

"I'm so glad the cook chose to make this," Lucy remarked. "I absolutely love duck. And it seems you do too, Angelica. The pleasure on your face is quite palpable."

Angelica could only nod and smile and sip her wine, even as her cheeks grew hotter.

She wasn't as surprised when the syllabub arrived for dessert as she'd been with the previous dishes, but she was equally grateful, for it tasted divine. Smooth, creamy, and just a touch tart. Exactly how she liked it.

"I might order Cook to prepare this every day from now on," Randolph murmured close to her ear when they filed out of the dining room later. As host, he'd stood by the door, allowing all the ladies to precede him, and since she'd been seated furthest from him, Angelica was the last to exit. He pressed his palm to her lower back while directing her into the parlor, infusing her with his heat and forcing a series of improper tingles to dart across her skin. "As long as there are no other men about to watch you eat."

She wasn't sure she understood his meaning. It seemed most peculiar, but his voice and his tone suggested he'd just alluded to something wicked or, at the very least, slightly naughty, though she'd no idea how food might factor in.

"It was delicious," she told him, not only because it was true but because his effort deserved to be acknowledged. "Thank you."

He merely bowed his head, then strode away to engage Miss Stevens in conversation. Angelica watched him go. While he might have singled her out for the meal, he was obviously aware that it would be bad form to make her the sole recipient of his attention. She smiled. He behaved like the perfect host, and in spite of their altercation last night, she was warming to him in a way she hadn't expected. Of course, the kiss might have helped as well in that regard. The mere memory of it had the ability to leave her feeling flummoxed.

Angelica searched the room for Lucy and started in her direction as soon as she spotted her. But she'd barely taken two steps before something soft and cold breezed across her shoulders. She flinched. It was almost as if some invisible person breathed cold air on her skin.

Stiffening, Angelica kept on moving. That rustling sound she'd heard before snuck up behind her, like hollow whispers demanding attention.

She turned.

Stared back.

Of course there was nothing.

There never was.

Swallowing hard, she told herself for what had to be the hundredth time that she was being silly. In such an old house, creaky floors and odd sounds were bound to occur. And just because she couldn't locate the draft, didn't mean it didn't exist.

"Are you all right?"

Angelica jumped, spun around, and pressed her palm to her breast when she spotted Lucy. "Heavens, you nearly startled the life out of me."

Lucy frowned. "You look awfully pale. Come, let's have some hot tea over there in the corner." They approached the small sofa they'd occupied the previous evening and helped themselves to the tea that sat waiting on the low oval table.

"You've been very jumpy all day. And frowny. Is something amiss?"

"No, no." Angelica sipped her tea. She willed her heart to slow but it kept pounding. And an awful sensation twisted deep in her belly – a queasiness that kept her on edge.

"Are you certain?" Lucy watched her too closely for comfort. "Is it Lord Sterling? Did he upset you somehow?"

Yes.

And no.

He'd frightened her last night and then today he'd swept her off her feet. Had any other woman in history ever been courted by a more contradictory man? No one confused her more, and nothing concerned her as much as the eeriness lurking within the walls of Colchester Hall. It seemed almost as if a presence existed – one she could not see or accurately define. But she could feel it, and it made her want to leave. Except she didn't have the heart to distress her mother. And at the same time, she was starting to believe she and Randolph could be happy together if they tried.

Did she really want to give up her chance of that just because his home made her feel uneasy?

"It's not Lord Sterling." His anger with her made sense. She shook her head, drank some more tea. She surveyed the room, then stopped when her gaze found Mrs. Essex. She stood near Randolph, issuing instructions to one of the maids, it seemed. Her gaze shifted and her cool blue eyes met Angelica's. The perfectly lovely smile she always wore materialized on her face. Angelica's skin pricked. "It's something else. Something's not right."

"What?"

Mrs. Essex stepped closer to Randolph and dipped her head toward him. They exchanged a few more words as a master and housekeeper might need to do, but there was a sense of familiarity between them that felt entirely wrong.

An ugly sensation flowed through Angelica's body. It slithered and stretched until it encompassed her heart and caused a sharp pang. She turned to Lucy with a start.

"Have you visited the gallery?"

Lucy blinked. "No."

"Would you like to?"

"Now?"

Angelica nodded. She wanted to leave this room and the nattering women all vying for Randolph's attention. She wished to forget Mrs. Essex existed and that she possessed the power to make her wonder and imagine the worst sort of things until she felt sick. But most of all, she had an unsettling urgency to see a particular portrait.

"Would you please slow down?" Lucy panted, clinging to the banister as they reached the top of the stairs. Their bedchambers were to the left, Randolph's somewhere off to the right, and the gallery...

"This way." Angelica hastened along the walkway bordering the perimeter of the stairwell. "It must be over here somewhere, toward the front of the house."

It was almost as if she were being pulled toward her destination. She stepped through a tall double door and went utterly still. This was it and for some strange reason she couldn't quite explain, the space demanded reverence.

Lucy must have felt it too, for she did not utter a word when she entered. She just sighed, ever so softly, and followed

Angelica down the long row of Sterling family portraits. Until they reached the end.

Angelica stared at the wall in disappointed silence. "It isn't here. The portrait of Lady Sterling should be right there." She pointed to the vacant spot in case Lucy needed explanation.

"Perhaps Lord Sterling found it too painful to look at and had it removed?"

Angelica sighed. "It's possible." For some peculiar reason she'd *needed* to see it. She couldn't explain why. It made no sense really, unless there was something...some indefinable manifestation beyond comprehension.

She dared not imagine, but what if the shift in the air and the cries for help had been no illusion, what if the shadows that seemed to flicker at the edge of her vision were really there? What if...

She sucked in a breath as the temperature dropped. The light from the wall sconces sputtered. A lonely wail clutched at her heart and stiffened her limbs.

"Lucy?"

"Hmm?"

Angelica gripped her friend's arm. "Do you hear that?"

Lucy tilted her head. "Hear what?"

"The plea for help," she whispered, glancing around, searching for something concrete she could point to as evidence.

Lucy laughed. "It's just the wind."

Angelica had thought so too. She'd convinced herself of it numerous times but she wasn't so sure any more. "We should return downstairs."

"After you made me almost run up here? I need a moment, and besides, now that we're here, don't you want to look at the rest of the portraits?"

She didn't, but she would humor her friend even though all she wanted was to climb into bed. Her teeth practically chattered and her toes had gone numb in her slippers. Why didn't Lucy feel the same way? Why didn't anyone?

"Ah. There you are." Mrs. Essex stood at the opposite end of the gallery. "You left the parlor without informing anyone of where you were going."

"We meant to come straight back once we'd taken a look at the portraits," Angelica said.

Mrs. Essex smiled as she always did, but this time there was a curious gleam in her eyes. "And did you find what you sought?"

"No," Lucy told her. "Lady Sterling's portrait is missing."

Mrs. Essex's lips stretched until her smile became an unnatural grimace. "So it is."

She said nothing more, offered no explanation or any other useful information. She just stood there. And waited.

"I think I'll retire for the evening," Angelica said.

"I thought you were going to return downstairs," Mrs. Essex remarked.

Angelica met her gaze and held it. "I changed my mind."

The housekeeper squinted. A little snort followed. "And what of you, Miss Harlow?"

"I will also retire," Lucy said loyally.

"Well. I shall make excuses for both of you then," Mrs. Essex said.

She departed, leaving Lucy and Angelica alone once more. "I really don't like her," Angelica murmured.

"Me neither. You will have to sack her once you and Lord Sterling have wed."

Angelica almost choked on the air she'd just inhaled. "You speak as if the matter has already been decided when I can assure you it has not. And please don't tell me you've given up trying to win him for yourself."

"He has eyes only for you, Angelica."

"That's not true," Angelica said even though she believed might be.

Lucy gave her a dubious look. "Let us be honest with one another, shall we?"

"Very well." Angelica linked her arm with Lucy's, and together they made their way back to their bedchambers. "It is possible you may have a small point."

"Oh really?"

"Well... He did kiss me."

Angelica spent the next half hour in Lucy's bedchamber, recounting every detail.

"I LIKE YOUR BONNET," Lady Seraphina told Angelica the next day.

They'd left Colchester Hall roughly ten minutes earlier to go for the walk Randolph had planned. He appeared to be exerting an effort with Miss Chesterfield, but her shyness made it near impossible for anyone to carry on a conversation with her. Angelica had tried during breakfast only to give up. She admired Randolph for his persistence and for doing his best to make sure none of his guests felt left out.

She eyed Lady Seraphina suspiciously. Lucy had kept her company until a few seconds ago when she'd hurried ahead to ask her mother about a particular plant she'd spotted.

"Thank you," Angelica said. "Yours is very stylish as well."

Lady Seraphina smirked. "I didn't say yours was stylish, only that I like it."

Angelica rolled her eyes. "Of course," she muttered. She glanced at Lady Seraphina and finally asked, "What do you want?"

"I do so love your forthright manner." Lady Seraphina's voice was light and breezy. It made Angelica gnash her teeth. "I think I shall try to be equally frank. You are quite obviously my only competition. The rest of that lot—" she waved her hand in the general direction of the other ladies who were walking ahead "—is hardly worth noting."

Angelica gaped at her. She could not believe her own ears or that anyone, least of all a *lady*, could be so indescribably rude. It was beyond the pale and so thoroughly shocking it took a full minute at least for Angelica to put her mind in order and find her tongue.

"That lot, as you so delicately refer to them, consists of well-bred ladies. Women of your own class." Angelica's hands had balled into fists. She was furious, practically shaking with it. "How dare you treat them as if they're beneath you?"

Lady Seraphina blinked. And then she laughed. "Because they are." She gave a little twist of her wrist. "Honestly, you cannot place a farmer's daughter on the same rung of the social ladder as I. Why, not even you have the same importance as I, but—"

"Miss Stevens' father is one of the wealthiest men in England. He is not a farmer, but an affluent landowner."

"Pfft..."

Dear God, she was going to have to strangle her, right here on this lovely hilltop. Angelica glanced at the steep decline to her left. There were brambles there. Just one little nudge and Lady Seraphina could be stuck in them. She grinned at the image of the other lady tumbling over the side, her feather-trimmed bonnet whipped from her head like a bird taking flight.

"Mind your step over here," Randolph yelled. "It's a little—"

"Well, it was lovely chatting with you," Lady Seraphina said, "but the time has come for me to take advantage."

Angelica wasn't sure what she was talking about and realized she didn't much care. She was simply glad to be rid of the woman who was now running forward, bustling her way past Miss St. James and Miss Stevens and practically elbowing her way to the front.

Lucy glanced back at Angelica as if to say, 'what's going on?' Angelica merely shrugged and kept on walking. She'd almost reached the others when a sudden gust of wind swept past her, whipping her gown around her ankles. She stumbled against the force of it.

"Be careful," Randolph warned. "No! Wait!"

A scream sliced the air. Angelica blinked and looked toward the rest of the group. And then she gripped her skirts and ran forward. "What happened?"

"I'm not sure," Lucy told her.

Together, they moved past the women blocking their view. A strange ball of emptiness grew in the pit of Angelica's stomach. She stepped forward, her gaze following the path that descended to the vast blanket of heather below. Randolph was making his way down as quickly as he could manage, his long legs carrying him toward the spot where Lady Seraphina lay in a crumpled heap.

"Goodness," Angelica muttered. She'd imagined this very scenario just a few minutes before, but surely... No. It was just a coincidence. The wind had come and Lady Seraphina had been hastening forward. She simply must have lost her balance.

"Her parents will have my head," Lady Seraphina's chaperone complained. "Oh heavens, they'll sack me right on the spot."

"Now, now," Rose told her in that soothing voice she'd used on Angelica so often when she'd been a child. "The wind caught her unawares, that's all."

Angelica frowned. The air was completely still.

She glanced back at Colchester Hall and froze.

There, framed by the curtains in her bedchamber window, was a woman. Mrs. Essex perhaps? It was too far to tell. She blinked, and when she opened her eyes again, the woman had gone.

"I have to get her back to the house," Randolph said, startling Angelica as he passed her with Lady Seraphina in his arms.

"O—of course," Angelica said even though she was fairly certain he hadn't been addressing her alone. She swallowed and did her best to stem the unnatural foreboding that twined itself around her.

"You look unnerved," Lucy remarked. "She'll be all right, you know. I believe it's just a sprained ankle."

"Yes," Angelica muttered, forcing a smile. "There's nothing to be concerned about." Repeatedly, her gaze drifted back to her bedchamber window as they walked toward the house. It remained empty, devoid of movement and life.

RANDOLPH WAS IN A SIGNIFICANTLY better mood the following day when he escorted the young ladies into the village. According to the physician he'd sent for, Lady Seraphina had only sprained her ankle and simply needed to rest. Her health was not in any danger, but he would at least be saved from having to suffer her company. Instead, he'd allow himself the satisfaction of pursuing Angelica.

With this in mind, Randolph deliberately snuck between her and Miss Harlow and offered each an arm. Miss Harlow grinned and her eyes sparkled with mischief, suggesting she knew precisely what he was about. With luck, she'd prove a valuable ally in his attempt at courtship.

Angelica on the other hand was surprisingly demure today. Unlike herself. Only the ghost of a smile graced her lips as she glanced up to acknowledge his presence, and uncomfortable looking creases marred her forehead.

"I must commend you," he said, deciding to start with a compliment. "It was good of you to defend Miss Stevens yesterday."

Her lips parted. Surprise widened her eyes. "You heard?"

"We all did," Lucy chimed in. She quickly bit her lip. "Sorry. I should have mentioned it."

A lovely blush flooded Angelica's cheeks. She directed her gaze forward. "I couldn't keep silent. To do so would have gone against my moral compass."

"I know," Randolph said. He dipped his head a bit closer to hers and added, "Yet another reason why you have gained my regard." Her blush deepened and he mentally marked the moment as a small victory. "While I did suggest visiting the teashop and haberdashery, I would like to stop by the bookshop for a quick look."

"Oh." The singular word – more of an exclamation, really – popped out of Angelica's mouth with startling rapidity.

Randolph smiled. He hadn't known she was fond of reading. It wasn't something they'd discussed. But it pleased him to know they shared a common interest, for he simply adored books – loved the smell of them, the feel of them, the knowledge crammed between their pages.

"I'll just inform the others in case they'd like to join us." Randolph did so, but the rest of the ladies were far more interested in shopping for trimmings, though Lady Bloomfield did consider his invitation for a moment. She changed her mind, however, when Mrs. Harlow pointed out that their daughters would have each other for chaperones.

"Is there a particular genre you favor?" Randolph asked once they'd stepped inside the overcrowded shop. Books lay everywhere: stacked on counters and practically bursting from shelves. It was perfect.

"Poetry," Miss Harlow told him. "I'm especially fond of Robert Burns and poems written in his style."

Randolph wasn't surprised. There was a softness about most of Burns's poems that made for light and uplifting reading. They weren't the tormented writings of some tortured soul, determined to convey his despair and heartache to the world.

"I've an excellent collection of his work right over here," the shopkeeper said. He led Miss Harlow between two bookcases.

"And how about you?" Randolph asked Angelica.

"Ordinarily..." She stopped herself and glanced about. "This is a lovely shop."

"I'm glad you think so. I've always had a particular fondness for books. They allowed me to pretend I was someone else. They offered escape."

"What were you escaping from?" She asked the question quietly, almost reverently, as if being given an insight to his soul truly mattered.

With anyone else, he would have ended the revelation there with a shrug of his shoulders and a flip answer. But not with her. She deserved better. "My brother is ten years younger than I. We never had much in common."

"Where is he now?"

"In Scotland, attempting to gain his independence, as he put it."

"And your parents?" she asked softly.

Randolph grimaced. "My father woke up one day and decided he'd had enough of being an earl. Only a hastily written note left behind on his desk informed me he'd gone to America."

Her eyes widened. "Really?"

"He writes me every now and then. Usually when he's running low on funds." Randolph shifted his weight and propped one shoulder against the bookcase beside him. "Meanwhile my mother, the timid lady who lived in constant fear of his temper, used the occasion of his departure as an excuse to leave for France indefinitely."

"One could say you have something of a temper as well."

He knew she didn't mean the words as an insult, merely an observation, yet his skin still stretched and tightened while heat began rising to the top of his head. "Don't ever compare me to my father," he told her darkly, then swallowed and forced himself to relax upon noting her startled expression. Had he just proven her point? He sighed. "Again, I apologize for the other evening, especially if I frightened you. It really wasn't my intention but I cannot—"

"Shh... It's all right. It could not be helped."

His fingers flexed. "Nevertheless. I should have practiced greater control."

She stared at him and he stared back, their gazes locked. A moment passed, then two, three. "My preferred genre includes all things gothic," she suddenly blurted.

He almost laughed. It really couldn't be helped. She was so wonderfully surprising, he probably would have kissed her again if they'd been somewhere more private. Heaven only knew he'd been able to think of little else but that one kiss they'd shared since it had happened. Her response had been remarkable and the hunger he'd experienced... God, it was enough to drive a man mad.

He cleared his throat, allowed a crooked smile. "Then I would expect you to have a greater appreciation for my home than you do." It was meant as a joke of sorts, but she did not laugh or smile in response.

"The books I read tend to include supernatural occurrences and the macabre." Her voice faltered. She clasped her hands together. Swallowed. "While I enjoy such stories, I have no interest in experiencing them for myself."

"Of course not. Who would?"

She stared at him and he caught something in her eyes, something fleeting in her expression – a hint of interest almost entirely obscured by whatever uncertainty plagued her.

He cleared his throat. "Have you read *Northanger Abbey*?"

"By Miss Austen?" She scrunched her nose. "I'm not a big fan of romance."

He smiled. And then, because the shopkeeper and Miss Harlow were quite engrossed in a lengthy poetic discussion, he grabbed Angelica by her hand and pulled her toward the back of the shop.

She gasped. "What are you doing?"

"Trying to seduce you?" He glanced back over his shoulder at her. "What do you think? Perfect spot for it, is it not?"

The edge of her mouth twitched, her lips began quivering, and then, for the first time in two days, she actually laughed. The sound punched him squarely in his chest, and God help him if it didn't feel good or right. Whatever her worries might be, most likely pertaining to her mother's financial straits and her own need for marriage, perhaps with a touch of doubt relating to him, he'd convince her they were unfounded. They would be good together. They had to be because otherwise...

He supposed he could always travel to London, endure a Season while taking his time to select someone else. Except he didn't want anyone else. He wanted *her* – Lady Angelica with her lack of pretense and forthright honesty. A woman ready to champion those who could not defend themselves, who voiced her opinion without apology and kissed him back with fervor.

"Here we are," he said once they reached the part of the shop where they'd find the book he sought. Four bookcases stood between them and Miss Harlow, offering them the sort of privacy they ought not to be permitted. Still holding Angelica's hand, he placed it against the spine of the book he wanted her to select. "This is not the average romance novel. Indeed, it stands apart from all of Miss Austen's other works to the point where I dare say you'd find it intriguing."

Her gloved fingers traced the gold embossed title on the first volume. And then she glanced up at him with the sort of profound curiosity that threatened to either stop his heart or make it race faster. "Have you read it yourself?"

Lost in the depth of her golden eyes, he was only able to nod.

She blinked. Her lips parted as if she meant to say something more, but whatever was on her mind must have flittered away, leaving her standing there much as he, utterly still and very aware.

Slowly, lest he startle her into motion and ruin the moment, he raised his palm to her cheek. Her eyes fluttered shut and a sigh, so wrought with longing he knew he risked losing control, swept past her lips to tickle his wrist, right where the edge of his glove ended.

Randolph's chest tightened. "Angelica." He loved her name, loved the way it felt on his tongue as he spoke it and how it seemed to remind him of all that was good and right with the world.

One quick glance in Miss Harlow's direction, just to be sure there was no risk of being discovered, and then he kissed her, stealing her breath and inhaling her scent, reveling in the small moan of pleasure she made in her throat. God, how he wanted and Christ, how he needed. After more than two years of him not touching a woman, Angelica was warm and willing and utterly delicious.

Her one hand was still on *Northanger Abbey*, but the other... The other clutched at his arm, holding on fast as he moved in closer, sandwiching her between him and the bookcase until he could feel the entire length of her body pressing against him in just the right places.

He nipped her lower lip with his teeth, urging her to open for him and delighting in the taste of her the moment she did. Lord, he could kiss her for hours, days, months, years. Hell, he could kiss her forever without getting tired.

"Angelica, you really must come and see what I've found."

It was Miss Harlow. Her voice, louder than necessary, forced Randolph to take a step back. "You should join her."

"Yes." She blinked in rapid succession.

He smiled, dropped his hand, and forced himself to step aside. "I'm sure she called you for a good reason."

"Yes," she repeated as if slightly dazed.

How could he not feel ten feet tall when she reacted to him with such innocent wonder? A comforting warmth unfurled right over his heart. "You should go."

As if recalling herself, she snatched the volumes of *Northanger Abbey* from the shelf and hastened toward the front of the shop, arriving there right before her mother came through the door. "I bought some lovely pieces of lace," Lady Bloomfield said. She paused and Randolph imagined her looking around. "Where's Lord Sterling?"

"At the back somewhere," Miss Harlow informed her. "I'm sure he'll join us once he's ready."

Randolph smiled to himself. He'd known he could count on her helping him out. Grabbing the book he'd come to purchase – a new account of Egyptian relics – he approached the ladies with what he hoped looked like an amicable smile.

The last thing he wished was for Lady Bloomfield to notice the desperate desire he felt for her daughter or to suspect they'd just been kissing. Not because he minded the repercussions. He meant to marry Angelica; his mind was firmly made up. But he sensed she needed more time to adjust, time to understand what was happening between them, and time to realize that he could fulfill her every need and make her gloriously happy. She would not appreciate being forced into something she wasn't yet sure of.

"I hope you like strawberry tarts," he said once they'd finished making their purchases. "The teashop I mentioned serves the best I've ever tasted."

"I gather you have a sweet tooth, my lord?" The question was posed by Lady Bloomfield.

Randolph discreetly brushed his fingers against Angelica's, grabbing them only briefly before releasing them once again and adding distance. "There are some confections I cannot resist."

Angelica's cheeks turned a bright shade of red. She gave him a chastising look, but all he could do was grin. He was enjoying himself far too much and considering the kiss they'd just shared, he wasn't sure he'd be able to manage a serious demeanor even if his life depended on it.

"WHAT WILL YOU DO?" Lucy asked Angelica the following afternoon. They'd been divided into groups of four—she was with Lucy and both their mothers— and were presently on their way to the music room in search of their next clue. While Angelica did not like Mrs. Essex, she had to give her credit for creating a well-planned treasure hunt. The riddles required a great deal of thought to solve them.

"About what?" Angelica and Lucy trailed behind, allowing their mothers to hurry ahead like eager young girls. It was quite entertaining to watch, and it allowed Angelica and Lucy to speak more privately with each other.

"Lord Sterling, of course. He will ask you to stay and then he will ask you to be his wife. Have you decided on your answer yet?"

Angelica sighed. She gave her friend a tentative look. "I'm not certain. On one hand, I must marry him for my mother's sake, but on the other I do not wish to remain here one day longer than necessary."

"I don't know why you dislike this house so much. Most women would be honored to call it their home. But whatever your reason may be, does it really matter where you live as long as you're getting *him*? Is he not worth sacrificing your taste in a home?"

Angelica gave her a deadpan stare. "I'm not in love with him, Lucy. It's a bit too soon to be speaking of sacrifices and such."

"Are you sure? That look in your eyes yesterday when we left the bookshop—"

Angelica cleared her throat. They'd entered the music room and the last thing she wanted was for her mother to be provided with additional reasons for getting Angelica to the altar. At least not until she'd made up her mind about what she wanted for herself and figured out her options. If there was even more than one to consider.

Thankfully, Lucy fell silent and broke away from Angelica in order to help search for the next clue. They eventually found it inside the piano and, upon deciphering it, headed toward the conservatory.

"Do you think you could grow to love him?" Lucy asked when they were once again able to speak discretely.

"I do not know." Or so she told herself, but the truth... The truth was she feared she might already be on her way to losing her heart and... "I cannot risk it. Not yet."

Not until she understood what she was getting herself into.

Lucy grinned, oblivious to Angelica's turmoil. "I'm not sure love is something one can control. You simply...fall."

This was followed by a sigh – an extremely telling one.

"My goodness," Angelica murmured. Lucy's lack of interest in Randolph suddenly made so much sense. "Who is he?"

"What?" Lucy glanced about quickly, her eyes no longer glazed over with longing but sharpened by panic.

Angelica drew a bit closer to her friend and lowered her voice to an almost inaudible whisper. "Who are you in love with?"

A wash of red colored Lucy's cheeks. She stammered a bit, then managed to compose herself and say, "Mr. Elliot Thompson. He is a friend of my brother's. But it hardly signifies since he has never shown any interest in me."

"Oh, but he must. I do not see how he cannot."

Lucy smiled. "You're very kind, but the truth is I always turn into a bashful ninny whenever he's near. As you know, I'm already soft spoken and shy, but with him... Dear lord, it's so much worse."

Angelica pondered that for a moment. Clearly Lucy would need some help opening Mr. Thompson's eyes. "We will find a way," she promised. "Somehow, you shall have the man you want, Lucy."

Because really, what was the point if someone as sweet and kind as her friend could not have her happily ever after?

"And what about you?"

Angelica tried to ignore the shift in the air and the chilling embrace that followed. She still hadn't figured out who had been at her bedchamber window the previous day, but a definite unpleasantness permeated Colchester Hall. It hung in the air like a damp smell, clinging to the walls in various shades of grey.

Of course, no one but she could see it or feel it, and that was perhaps the worst part of all.

The chill curled over her shoulders and slid down her arms. The soles of her feet felt damp. She glanced down and took a step back. Where were her stockings and shoes? Why was she barefoot and why...

Trembling from head to toe, she stared at the frozen ground, at the hem of her gown, no longer made from light green cotton but white and breezy, like a nightgown.

She sucked in a breath as a hard gust of wind whipped her back. Her hand curled around something crisp. Letters. Dozens of them fell from her hands until she was just clasping one.

I saw what happened. Meet me at midnight, by the entrance to the east wing if you want my help – a friend.

The cold sank into her bones, intensifying in strength until she cried out in pain. "Help me." But her voice was too weak. The wind so strong it swallowed it up. She staggered forward and fell. Her hand reached for the door and her nails raked helplessly over the wood. "Help me."

Her breaths faltered until just a wheezing hoarseness remained. Her heartbeats slowed, the pain subsided. A lock of red hair curled over her shoulder as she slumped sideways against the exterior wall. Her vision blurred until all she saw was the white misty air of her last exhalation.

A hand clasped her arm. "Angelica?" It was Lucy and she was shaking her hard.

Angelica gasped, drawing in air as if she'd been drowning. She stared at Lucy whose face filled with concern. "What happened?"

"I've no idea. You stopped walking and didn't respond when I spoke. It was almost as if you weren't there." Lucy shuddered and glanced around. "Is everything all right?"

"Yes. I think so." Still reeling from shock, Angelica prayed her friend would believe her so she could move on, avoid additional questions, and figure out what was happening to her without being labeled mad. "I just have to speak with Lord Sterling."

Now, more than ever, she had to uncover the truth.

Chapter Five

Seated behind his desk in his study, Randolph considered Mrs. Essex's words. Perhaps it had been unwise of him to request her opinion, but his butler was an elderly man who always said what he thought Randolph wanted to hear and his valet... Well, he was no better. So he'd turned to his housekeeper as a last resort.

"It is not that I find them unsuitable," she added with that pleasant smile she always wore. "Rather, I worry they won't make you happy."

He appreciated her concern, even though he believed she was wrong. "I think there's a chance Lady Angelica might."

Her eyes held his. "Is she not a bit too unpolished for the position?"

Randolph couldn't help but laugh. "You speak as though we're looking to hire a new servant." Although to be fair, he had made it sound much the same in his invitation.

"Well, the process you've chosen is not so very different, is it?"

He instantly sobered. "No. I don't suppose it is." He'd been interviewing the women, judging them, taking his time to carefully gauge compatibility. Only two had shown potential:

Miss Harlow and Lady Angelica, with Lady Angelica as the clear winner.

"Perhaps I am wrong about her. Although..." She sighed and dropped her gaze. Her smile slipped a little.

"Although what?"

Looking uncharacteristically uncertain, Mrs. Essex glanced back up. "She was in the gallery the other night."

"And?"

"She wanted to see your wife's portrait."

Numbness, starting at his fingertips, spread up his arms and reached inside his chest. "Curiosity is a natural thing." His voice sounded hollow even to his own ears.

"I don't think she will relent until she has all the answers."

His jaw tightened and his teeth clenched. "What answers?"

Mrs. Essex drew back, visibly surprised. "Forgive me. It is a sensitive subject and I... I did not mean to overstep."

"You should go." He knew his voice was harsh and he knew he was being unfair when all she was trying to do was help him, to warn him.

Something disturbing flickered within her blue eyes. There, then gone. She'd composed herself completely. Her smile was back in place. "Very well, my lord. I shall leave you to ponder your decision."

Randolph leaned back in his chair and did precisely that. Angelica was inquisitive and direct. She liked to know things and if she suspected there might have been foul play involved in his wife's death, she'd want to look into it. She'd want to know every detail.

Steepling his fingers, he considered the possible dilemma she posed. If she were his wife, would she stand by his side and protect his secrets, or turn him in for murder?

A gentle knock at the door drew him out of his reverie. "Enter!"

It was she. The woman who filled his every thought, the one he wanted to make his own. He stood in order to greet her.

"Angelica. Is everything all right?"

She looked strange. There was a haunted look about her, an eerie disquiet.

"Where's your wife's portrait?" Her voice was precise, calm, completely at odds with her expression. "It is not in the gallery. I've already looked."

His gut roiled with ominous concern. Every muscle in his body tightened to the point of snapping. "Why do you ask?" He ground out the words without any finesse.

"Because I want to see it." She glared at him, her eyes hard and determined.

Randolph tried to breathe. He tried to tamp down the rising panic. Each thump of his heart sent a painful jab straight through his chest. "It's in the attic," he managed. "I packed it away for a reason."

"Because her death broke your heart." He almost laughed. Yes, it had broken his heart all right, though not for the reason she thought but rather for countless others. "It must have been terribly difficult," she continued, "but it wasn't your fault. It was—"

"Stop." He couldn't bear anymore. "Is seeing the portrait a stipulation?"

She didn't hesitate. "Yes."

He didn't understand her reasoning, but it hardly mattered, did it? If seeing Katrina's likeness was what it would take, then so be it. He grabbed an oil lamp and lit it. The flame lurched to life. "Come with me."

FOR REASONS SHE COULD not begin to fathom, Angelica sensed she was pushing the bounds of what Randolph was willing to accept on her account. It made sense, she supposed. If he'd loved Katrina as much as she thought he had, then her death must have been truly devastating. Just the thought of her out there alone, freezing to death while he remained ignorant, unable to help. It must have been awful.

But after her vision, for she knew not what else to call it, she wished to look upon the face of the woman who'd been so dear to him. She wasn't sure what she hoped to accomplish by it, but perhaps the painting would offer some insight. Maybe seeing Randolph's wife would let her know whether the woman was seeking her help or attempting to chase her away.

A shudder scraped her spine. She didn't believe in ghosts but neither could she explain the strange encounters she'd been having or why no one else felt or saw the same things she did. Angelica glanced over her shoulder. The candles in the wall sconces flickered. Icy air curled around her ankles. Oblivious, Randolph marched ahead with clipped footsteps. His posture was rigid and utterly devoid of the warmth he'd shown toward her during the previous days. If anything, his demeanor was wrought by a carefully held control she feared might turn into full-blown anger if she wasn't careful. Her heart beat faster, not so much with the fear of the unknown this time but because she worried that being alone with this man might be very unwise.

"Perhaps we should do this some other time," she tried. "My mother ought to come with us. Or Lucy."

Ignoring her, he pulled a key from his pocket and unlocked a door at the end of the hallway. "I want this over and done with." The door opened with a creak to reveal a winding stone staircase. Randolph waited. He arched a brow. "Well?"

"I, um..." She looked around to make sure no one watched.

"It won't take long. If anyone chooses to search for you, you'll merely tell them you went exploring. It is a large house after all."

"Yes. I suppose it is."

When she still didn't budge he leaned forward. "This was your idea. *You* insisted I show you the portrait."

"Of course." She didn't like his tone or the way he acted. It was menacing. Harsh. The opposite of what she wished in a husband. But since he did have a point and she wasn't the sort to back down, she stepped forward into the stairwell.

A musty smell filled her nose. The door clicked shut. Randolph's large, imposing body warmed her back. Lifting the hem of her skirt so she would not trip, she started up the stairs. The soles of their shoes scraped the edge of each step. Their creeping shadows, pinned to the wall by the oil lamp's light, were unnaturally tall, willowy shapes that would feel right at home in one of those gothic novels she favored.

Angelica winced but kept going. She'd asked for this. The time for playing the coward was long gone now. Oh, if only she could trade places with Lady Seraphina. A sprained ankle and plenty of bed rest seemed like heaven compared with facing the mysteries of Colchester Hall while being subjected to Randolph's temper.

They reached the top and moved forward, away from the stairs and across rough, un-sanded floorboards. The wood creaked loudly beneath their feet while the flickering flame from the lamp danced across the underside of the roof. Angelica looked up, impressed by the intricate, interconnected joists and rafters. The light faded and she realized Randolph had left her behind. She quickened her pace, weaving her way between boxes, crates, and the odd piece of furniture.

There he was, just up ahead. Angelica's heart leapt. She could feel the darkness trying to catch her – the cold that started below in the hallway increasing its hold. Her teeth began to chatter. She folded her arms across her chest, hugging herself. Of course there would be no heat up here. They were practically out of doors. But what surrounded her was something deeper, stronger, a bleak desperation shrouded in ice.

"Here it is." Randolph spoke, his voice oddly detached.

Angelica moved to his side. He held the lamp high so the light fell directly upon a rectangular object. It sat on the floor, leaning against a post. A sheet was draped over it, not with care but with what appeared to have been a hasty attempt at concealment.

"Well?"

Angelica started. She glanced at him, uncertain of how to proceed.

He did not look at her, just stared straight ahead as if trying to brace himself for what was to come. "You will have to do it."

He turned to her then with raven-black eyes. A muscle twitched at the edge of his mouth. His features had never looked harder nor he more dangerous.

This was not a heartbroken man. The realization struck Angelica with such force she almost gasped. All this while, she'd thought he'd hidden the portrait because it pained him to be reminded of his loss. But that wasn't it at all.

His cutting tone, the tension of his jaw, and his overall posture were further proof of what she'd been too blind to see. She swallowed as realization cemented itself in her conscience.

If Randolph had once loved his wife as he'd claimed, then he no longer did. Instead, he hated her with every fiber of his being.

"I'm sorry," Angelica muttered, because it seemed like the most appropriate thing. And then, bolstering herself, she reached out and whipped the sheet aside.

The woman who looked back was stunning. She'd been blessed with a heart-shaped face, a creamy complexion, a perfectly proportioned nose, lips graced by a coy little smile, and eyes in a vibrant shade of cornflower blue.

Stillness overwhelmed Angelica. She sucked in some air, reminded herself to breathe. The chill in her bones snapped, sending pain into each of her joints. She hugged herself tighter.

"Satisfied?" Randolph stood rigidly beside her, his sneer of disdain shaking the air.

And all Angelica could think to say was, "Nobody told me her hair was red."

He turned to her, his expression grim and... She wasn't sure what. Surprised, didn't quite fit and yet she sensed his incomprehension.

Angelica stared at him, past him, to a spot just a short way away. Her mouth opened and closed, producing a senseless stammer. She wanted to speak but words wouldn't come. It felt like her lungs were being crushed because...

Because...

She could not voice it, could only stare.

"My God." Randolph turned more fully toward her. With jerky movements he tore off his jacket and flung it across her shoulders. His arms reached around her waist, lifting her up and against his chest, carrying her toward the stairs, then down, back to the hallway and into her room. Settling her on her bed, he bundled her up in her blanket. "I'll fetch your mother and ask the maids to draw a hot bath." His palm touched her forehead. "Christ, Angelica, you should have told me you were so cold."

He started to leave but she reached out and grabbed him. "Ra...ra...ndolph." Her body was violently shaking, her teeth clanging together, but this was important. She had to tell him. "I... I sa...saw her."

Randolph nodded. Just once. "I know."

Except he didn't. How could he when she was incapable of explaining. "I... I'm no...not talking ab...about the po...portrait."

He stilled. His eyes sharpened. For a second she thought he'd respond, but then he just unclenched her hand from his wrist and settled it in her lap. "You're overset, Angelica, and possibly in danger of getting terribly sick. I must do what I can to prevent that and you must rest."

"But..."

"We'll discuss this later."

He left and Angelica sank back against her pillows with a quivering moan of despair. Tears pricked her eyes, not because she was cold or frightened, but because she had no idea how she'd ever convince her mother or Lucy or Randolph she hadn't gone mad.

But the truth was that Lady Sterling was not at rest. Angelica still didn't know what her ghost wanted, but she'd finally seen her, standing behind Randolph's right shoulder and reaching forward in desperation.

"Mama?" Rose was bustling around the room when Angelica woke the next morning, arranging flowers that must have been brought in while she was sleeping.

Rose turned. "Lord Sterling cut these himself." Her eyes twinkled with girlish delight. "Aren't they stunning? They're from the conservatory."

She pressed her lips together as if to stop a bright smile, only to fail. Her hand covered her mouth to hide her laughter. "Lady Seraphina is quite put out by his fondness for you."

Her mother's good cheer was overwhelming, coming on the heels of what had been a dramatic day. Thankfully, the entity trying to communicate with her had offered her a reprieve. She'd experienced only comfort and warmth during her bath, and rather than being forced downstairs for dinner, she'd been allowed to enjoy a tray in bed while Lucy kept her company. It had been nice. Peaceful and pleasant.

Angelica blinked. "Lady Seraphina is back on her feet?"

Rose nodded. "Not even a broken leg would be able to keep her from going to the ball this evening. But she is doing better although I personally think she's silly for not accepting the cane Mrs. Essex offered to lend her." She sat on the edge of Angelica's bed and looked straight into her eyes. A frown wrinkled her brow. "I'm more concerned with you, however. Tell me, how are you feeling?"

"Perfectly well."

"Venturing into the attic alone was not the wisest decision, Angelica. Not only because you weren't dressed for the cold but because you were obviously snooping." Rose shook her head. "Whatever were you hoping to find?"

It was a good thing Lucy had mentioned the lie Randolph had fabricated in order to protect her reputation. It allowed Angelica to be prepared and able to keep the surprise from her face while her mother spoke. Apparently, she had found the attic door unlocked and had gone exploring. Randolph had happened upon her shivering form in the hallway when he'd gone to fetch his spectacles from his bedchamber.

Spectacles.

The thought of him occasionally requiring the assistance they offered was curiously endearing.

"Angelica?"

She forced herself to focus on her mother. What had she asked? She searched her brain until she located the answer. "The portrait of Lady Sterling. It was missing from the gallery."

Rose stared at her in bafflement. "You're lucky Lord Sterling's not angry with you for abusing his hospitality. Honestly, Angelica. What were you thinking?"

"I don't suppose I was," Angelica murmured. "I'm sorry, Mama. I was only trying to sate my curiosity. That's all."

"Well." Her mother huffed out a breath, then patted Angelica on her hand. "It's a good thing his lordship has taken a liking to you." She glanced at the flowers and smiled. "I'm certain you'll be the one he invites to stay on." There was no denying her joy, for it spilled from her like soap bubbles from a bath. "A proposal of marriage is close at hand, Angelica. Mark my word."

Unwilling to ruin her mother's good mood with her own doubts for the future, Angelica merely smiled. "I'd like to speak with him. With Lord Randolph, that is. If possible."

"Of course. I'll ask him to come and visit with you right away." Rose stood and smoothed her gown, assured Angelica she would return promptly, and departed.

A breakfast tray soon appeared, delivered by a maid. Rose returned to keep her company while she ate and then, half an hour later, there was a firm knock at her bedchamber door. Rose stood and went to greet Randolph.

"I'll be just in there," she said, pointing toward her own bedchamber. At Randolph's nod, she departed through the connecting door, leaving it so slightly ajar it might as well have been fully shut.

Angelica twitched her nose. Her mother was not exactly being subtle, though it did work to Angelica's advantage since she didn't want to share the words she meant to impart with anyone other than Randolph.

"You look much recovered," he said once he'd crossed the floor to her bedside. His hand reached out, hovered briefly as if with indecision, then took hold of hers.

A shock of awareness raced up her arm. Her pulse leapt and her gaze met his. His features relaxed before her eyes, softening, until the tension that had bracketed his mouth disappeared. He smiled and sat in the chair her mother had vacated when he arrived.

"I slept well," Angelica told him. His thumb brushed the back of her hand, tracing a circular path. Heat poured through her. "Thank you for the flowers. They were a lovely surprise."

"It occurred to me while selecting them that I wasn't sure of your tastes." A hint of irritation shadowed his words. "Most women like roses but they felt all wrong when I thought about you."

"The bouquet you put together is perfect. I'm especially fond of sunflowers." He'd mixed the happy blooms with a complementary assortment of sapphire blue asters and white chrysanthemums.

"I'm glad." He sounded immensely pleased.

Angelica bit her lip. The time had come for her to broach a most unusual subject. "Last night," she began, searching for words as she went along. "I discovered something important."

He raised an inquisitive eyebrow. The corner of his mouth lifted. "That you ought to dress warmer?"

She shot him a disgruntled look. "No." She shook her head. "This is about your wife."

His hand flinched, but he did not retrieve it. Not yet. "You asked to see the portrait. It was a condition, if you recall, and I complied. I have no wish to discuss her further. Not with you or with anyone else."

"That may well be," Angelica said, "but I cannot so easily ignore her. Not when she keeps demanding my attention."

His eyes searched her face and he suddenly brought her hand to his lips, kissing her skin with reverence. "You think me still in love with her. You worry you'll have to compete against her for my affections, but I assure you, Angelica, that's not the case."

"I know," she whispered. "Your hatred for her was etched on your face last night when you looked at her image. It could not have been any clearer."

"And you wish to know the reason." He spoke with pain and a touch of resentment, though she wasn't sure if it was aimed at her or at his wife. Angelica squeezed his hand. He took a deep breath. "You must forgive me, for this is not an appropriate story for an innocent young lady such as yourself, though I do believe circumstance demands honesty on my part." Turning his head, he met her gaze boldly. "I learned my wife was unfaithful to me the same day she died. She'd complained of a headache the night before, excusing herself from her wifely duties. When I went to check on her in the morning, I discovered her lover, asleep by her side."

Angelica gasped in shock. "Dear God."

"She denied any wrongdoing when I questioned her, which only made me angrier since the evidence was right there, staring me in the face." A disgusted snort punctuated the sentence. "After tossing the groom out, for God help me *that* was the man she'd decided to lay with, I informed her that she would be promptly removed to Fennly House – a property of mine in York – where she would live out the rest of her life alone." His breaths came in short little bursts and he now gripped her hand hard. "Her betrayal broke my heart, but at least it opened my eyes to the truth. I just wish I..."

His words fluttered off into obscurity.

After a number of seconds, Angelica quietly prodded, "What?"

He started. Blinked. His expression hardened, not with anger this time but with pain. "She died because of me. It's only fair to tell you the truth so you don't get trapped with a monster. For that is what I am. If it weren't for me, Katrina would still be alive."

Angelica stared at him. Hard. She didn't believe him for a second, no matter how convinced he was of what he'd just told her. "How?" A straightforward question with no room for ambiguity.

A lost gaze collided with hers. "Things were said. Despicable things." His voice faltered. "Had she not feared me, had she not run..." He was shaking.

"You are not to blame." Angelica's voice was firm. Whatever had truly transpired, whether his wife had cuckolded him or something more sinister was at play, Randolph wasn't at fault. "Any other man in your position would have done as you did. Your reaction is perfectly understandable."

"Angelica." Her name carried a world of doubt with it.

"No. Wait. There's something I must tell you, something you will not want to accept but... If you give me a chance to explain, it may shed new light on what happened."

His eyebrows drew together. "I'm not sure I follow."

Angelica took a deep breath. "Your wife's soul is restless, Randolph. I don't know why, but she's not at peace. I think—"

"What are you saying?" His voice had dropped so low she could barely hear him.

Angelica plowed ahead, undaunted. "She's been communicating with me from the beyond. She's—"

He shot to his feet and stepped back so abruptly he almost knocked over the chair. His eyes were wide, his expression one of stark disbelief. "Is this a joke to you? A game perhaps?"

"No. Of course not. It is a serious matter." She struggled to sit up straighter. "Your wife—"

"Was a whore. An adulteress. An outright liar who pretended to love me when clearly she didn't."

"Perhaps. Perhaps not. Randolph, something's not right, I can feel it."

"Oh you can, can you?" His mocking tone took her aback even though she'd known to expect it. After all, she herself had dismissed all the sounds and sensations even though she had experienced them for herself. It wasn't until the vision that she'd allowed herself to believe. "Is it perhaps your attempt at making up stories about the impossible that seems a bit off? Ghosts don't exist, Angelica. Shame on you for supposing I might believe such claptrap."

The air instantly cooled. Angelica caught a swift movement out of the corner of her eye. She turned her head. "See that? The way the curtain is moving?"

"A draft is most likely to blame." Annoyance dripped from every word. "Christ, what a fool I have been."

"No. Please." She held her hand toward him. "Randolph, you have to believe me. You have to—"

"No." He slashed the air with his arm. "Good God, you sound just like her, begging for me to have faith in something that obviously isn't true. Does my forehead have 'gullible' written upon it in big bold letters?"

"Of course not."

His mouth flattened and his eyes hardened to shards of flint. "I want you gone," he said with low and deadly precision. "Pack your bags and leave. Immediately." He turned for the door.

Angelica squared her shoulders and straightened her spine. "No."

He halted, his hand on the handle. Slowly, he turned back to face her. "You plan to defy me?"

"If necessary. Yes." She pulled back the covers and climbed from the bed. He should not see her like this, clad only in her nightgown. It wasn't appropriate and yet she had no choice but to go to him. "I will not leave you. Not like this. Not while you need me."

His eyes flashed and his nostrils flared. "Never presume to know what I need."

She tipped her chin up. "Fine." She gave him her best glare. "But perhaps you should ask yourself if it is possible for me to go mad within a few days. Think back to our conversations, Randolph. Consider your foremost reason for having an interest in me."

A nerve ticked in his cheek, tugging at the edge of his mouth. He stared back at her in silence until he finally said, "You speak your mind with unvarnished honesty."

"I do not lie."

"And yet I would be a fool to believe you."

"You seek proof. Validation." Her mind raced. If the roles were reversed would she believe him? Probably not. She hadn't even believed herself until her eyes had confirmed what her mind suspected. *Think*. There had to be something – a piece of information she couldn't possibly know unless she was being honest. Her mind cleared and she suddenly remembered. "Katrina was holding a letter and..." Angelica paused, tried to focus. Her brow wrinkled. "There was a ring, I believe. A gold band with leaves clasping a bright green emerald. And a scar – tiny, but visible – right between her thumb and index finger."

"How can you know this?" His hands clasped her shoulders, shaking her slightly. Wild eyes filled with confusion bored into hers. "How can you possibly know this?"

"Because I was there. Yesterday, before the attic, for just a brief moment I was transported. I do not know how, it still seems impossible, but I was her and I was freezing to death outside while clutching a letter."

"What did it say?" The question was slowly exhaled.

"I..." Angelica shook her head, closed her eyes, thought back. The script was a blurry haze that slowly came back into focus. "I saw what happened." She gulped down a lungful of air. "I saw what happened. Meet me at midnight by the entrance to the east wing if you want my help." Somehow, her hand found his. "It was signed by *a friend*."

"It isn't possible." But his tone was different than earlier and he did not pull away from her this time. "I burned that letter myself. You cannot have seen it."

"I know. It defies explanation."

He stared past the side of her face, his eyes fixed on some point far in the distance. "You said you saw her." His eyes snapped back to hers. "Last night after the attic, you told me you saw her. My wife. I thought you meant the painting but..." Incredulity pulled at his eyebrows, drawing them together until a crease appeared between them. He shook his head. "That's not what you were referring to. Is it?

A blossom of hope bloomed inside her. "She was standing roughly two yards behind you, her hand outstretched while clasping the letter."

"What does she want?"

"I have no idea yet, but it stands to reason that she either wants to frighten me away or seek my help."

Swallowing, he allowed his gaze to roam the room. "Is she here now?"

"I don't believe so."

He clenched his jaw and nodded. For the briefest moment his hand squeezed hers, then released it. He pinched the bridge of his nose then looked at her – really looked at her until she felt her cheeks flame. Dressed in only her nightgown and reminded of all it revealed, her inhibitions returned in full force.

"You ought to get back into bed, *my lady*."

Angelica scrambled back to the safety of her blankets and hastily flung them over herself. *My lady*. The way he'd said it... Her heart raced in response to what it implied. Once she was comfortably settled, he returned to the chair by her side and sat.

"I hope you can forgive my initial reaction to what you have told me. Instinct commanded me to treat it as a deception." He bowed his head, allowing his black locks to fall forward over his brow. "Thank you for making me listen – for standing up to me and what you believe in. You're brave, Angelica. Most women in your position would have run screaming from this house by now."

"Don't think I didn't consider it," she muttered with a wry twist of her lips.

He started to smile, but seemed to remember something that stopped it from fully forming. "Then why have you stayed?"

Angelica glanced across at the flowers. "Because I'm starting to think this might be where I belong."

His eyes darkened in contrast to the gentle caress of his fingers as they tugged a stray lock of hair behind her ear. "God, I want to kiss you right now."

Her lips parted with surprise. "Moments ago you wanted to toss me out."

"Can you honestly blame me?"

She thought about that. Seriously. Her lips quirked. "No. I don't suppose I can."

Warmth, the kind that brought to mind cozy evenings spent in front of an open fire, emanated from his eyes. "Loath as I am to leave your side, I should probably go. Mrs. Essex has—"

"Randolph." Angelica clutched his hand. "I know she is one of your most trusted servants, but I don't feel comfortable in her presence. She unnerves me."

"If it is her beauty you're concerned with—" a quelling look silenced her protest "—you may rest assured that it has never had any effect on me. It would, however, be dishonest of me to deny an awareness of it."

"As comforting as that is for me to hear, it is not her appearance that concerns me but rather an unpleasant feeling I get whenever I'm near her."

"And you are certain it isn't because you fear she might tempt me, because I promise you, Angelica, you have nothing to fear on that score. Mrs. Essex is a servant, a young and attractive one, I'll grant you, but a servant nonetheless, and I am not the sort of man who would ever cross the line that exists between us. Even if I were interested, which I am not."

In her heart, she knew this to be true and yet the woman still intimidated her. Could she possibly doubt her judgment, and him, on account of her own insecurities? Maybe. She certainly didn't relish the idea of having a housekeeper who would forever outshine her. People would wonder, would they not, about her reason for keeping Mrs. Essex in her employ? They would ask, as she had done, if she was Randolph's mistress.

"If I stay and we marry, would you consider letting me hire a new housekeeper?"

"And sack Mrs. Essex?" Incredulity colored his words.

"I realize I'm probably being silly, but she and I would have to interact a great deal on a daily basis, and I simply cannot see myself doing so with a woman I do not like."

"Angelica, she is a widow with no other means of support. If I were to let her go, do you honestly think she would find employment elsewhere when this is the only job she has ever had?"

It was a rhetorical question of course, because any reasonable person would know that no other household would hire a housekeeper with Mrs. Essex's looks. Her presence would forever pose a threat to the lady of the house, effectively deeming her unemployable.

"Please trust my judgment when I tell you that she is a fine housekeeper," Randolph continued. He raised her hand to his lips and pressed a kiss to her skin. "And you have nothing to fear from her in the least. My devotion is to you."

His declaration melted Angelica's bones until she felt like a gooey mess. "Very well," she agreed when she was able to find her voice.

A smile spread across his face. "Get up and get dressed. I have a surprise waiting for you downstairs." He stood, crossed to the connecting door, and gave it a rap. Rose entered with enough of a delay to assure Angelica that her mother had not been listening in on their conversation. "Tonight we shall dance," he told Angelica, "and then there will be no doubt as to whom I have chosen."

Chapter Six

Music floated through the air, mixing with the dazzling glow from two magnificent crystal chandeliers. Gems—hanging from earlobes, dripping from wrists, and wound around necks—winked in response to the light. Feathers adorning fans and hairpieces alike bowed and swayed in time to a mutual rhythm. Never before had Angelica witnessed such opulence. Gowns cut in the latest styles and embellished with beadwork, ribbons, and gold thread embroidery shimmered in response to each movement made by the ladies who wore them.

And then there was Randolph. He was handsome on an ordinary day, but tonight? Dressed in all black evening attire, he'd stolen her breath when she'd seen him standing at the entrance to the ballroom. They hadn't had time to exchange many words since he was the host and thus duty-bound to receive the rest of his guests as well. But flames had danced in his eyes as he'd watched her approach, and his lips had brushed her ear when he'd leaned in to tell her how stunning she looked.

With her mother by her side, she'd murmured her thanks before moving away, her ice blue skirts swishing across the floor as she went. She'd even managed to ignore Mrs. Essex's challenging gaze as she'd passed her, allowing herself to focus solely on the enjoyment ahead. Today had offered no additional chills or inexplicable visions, granting Angelica a reprieve from the anxiousness that had chased her since her arrival at Colchester Hall.

"Isn't it magnificent?" Lucy asked when the two of them took a turn of the room later that evening. She and Randolph had already danced a country dance, and he was now partnering with Miss Stevens for a quadrille.

"It is indeed." Even the refreshment table was a vision to be marveled at with two large fruit pyramids crafted from strawberries, melons, orange slices, and pineapples standing at each end. Several trays containing triangle-shaped sandwiches, a couple of three-tiered displays piled with colorfully decorated petits fours, and large crystal bowls filled with punch and lemonade stood between them. Champagne was constantly being passed around by footmen while maids drifting between the guests offered bite-sized meals, each skewered by a beautifully carved toothpick.

"I shall miss you," Lucy added. "I do not have many friends and certainly none whose company I enjoy as much as yours. Promise you'll write?"

"Of course." Angelica smiled brightly to banish the maudlin mood Lucy's words encouraged. She would miss her as well. "I expect you to keep me updated on your Mr. Thompson."

Lucy flushed a deep shade of scarlet and quickly opened her fan to chase away the heat. "He's not *my* Mr. Thompson."

"Well, if you like him half as much as I think you do, he should be, if only to make you happy."

"You really are the truest friend and... Oh, it's Lord Sterling. I dare say he's coming toward us."

And so he was. His long legs cut a direct line through the crowd, effortlessly parting it as he made his approach. And then he was there, standing before Angelica, his dark eyes glittering like a pair of black diamonds.

"My lady." He held his hand toward her. "I believe it is time for our dance."

She did not hesitate. Not for a second. His fingers curled around hers, offering her security and, dare she hope, the promise of love? Her heart beat frantically as they made their way onto the dance floor. And then she was in his arms, swirling about, and it all felt...

Perfect.

"Angelica." Piercing intensity met her gaze as he spun her around. His hand pressed firmly against her back, guiding her along. "I know there is much for us to resolve, but I would be honored if you and your mother would remain here at Colchester Hall one more week."

He was formally voicing his intentions, asking her to make a decision. Of course, she'd already done so, in spite of her lingering concerns. On one hand, she would have to accept his ancestral home and the ghost that came with it, not to mention the constant presence of Mrs. Essex. On the other, her mother's home would be safe and... Well, then there was the man himself. She smiled up at him while reflecting on their brief acquaintance. He'd laughed with her, chastised her, doubted her, and finally placed his trust in her. He'd listened to her complaints and taken deliberate strides to please her, not only by catering to her preferred taste for food but by rearranging the formal parlor.

That had been the surprise he'd mentioned. When she'd come downstairs for luncheon, Lucy had shown her into the room which seemed completely transformed. Randolph had followed her advice to the letter, creating a cozy atmosphere in which she knew she would feel right at home.

And then, of course, there was his thoughtful selection of flowers and, most importantly, his acceptance of her as a person. He liked her boldness – encouraged it even – and always seemed to appreciate her company.

All in all, now that the time had come, her answer was easy. "Nothing would please me more."

A spark of pleasure brightened his eyes and his hand squeezed hers. "I'm incredibly glad to hear it."

"Did you doubt my response?"

"A little."

His uncertainty conveyed a startling degree of vulnerability. "Then allow me to reassure you. Now that my mind is made up, nothing will ever compel me to leave you. Unless it is what you want."

"I would never."

She believed him, yet the nature of their agreement forced her to say, "That is for you to decide within the next week."

"Angelica, I—"

"Take your time." She did not want him making a hasty decision. She needed him to be certain, because if he wasn't, she feared the obstacles they would face in the future as husband and wife might tear them apart. And that was something she would not be able to bear.

He frowned with distinct disapproval, yet he did as she asked. "Very well."

Angelica smiled as she savored the moment. Who would have thought it possible to fall in love within the space of one week? And yet she knew this was what she had done, for she could not imagine her life without Randolph in it. She craved his nearness and yes, his kisses, but also the conversations they would be able to have. He respected her and treated her as his equal, which was something none of the young men she'd met in London had ever been capable of. The moment she'd voiced her unfiltered views, they'd labeled her difficult, too opinionated for her own good.

Not Randolph. By contrast, he encouraged her to be direct and honest. It was liberating, really, and utterly wonderful.

The music faded, drawing them to a gliding halt. He bowed and she curtseyed as custom dictated, but instead of escorting her off the dance floor immediately after, Randolph clasped her hand in his and turned. Together, side by side, they faced his guests.

"Ladies and gentlemen." He spoke with impressive clarity. "As you know, I am looking to remarry. During this past week, I have considered several young ladies and am now pleased to confirm that my choice has been made. Lady Angelica has agreed to remain here at Colchester Hall for another week together with her mother, after which she'll receive my offer of marriage."

"Nooo!"

Angelica fought not to laugh in response to Lady Seraphina's shrill protest, which was quickly drowned out by clapping and cheers. Amidst the crowd were the rest of the candidates Randolph had invited. Most wore sullen expressions, except Lucy who openly grinned.

Angelica glanced up at the man she'd fallen in love with. The joy he conveyed with the curve of his lips and the heated gaze he was subjecting her to made her heart bloom with warmth. This was what happiness felt like, and with him by her side she believed it would last forever.

"Tomorrow morning will be busy," he told her later in reference to the rest of the guests' departure. With Rose's permission, Randolph had been allowed to walk Angelica to her bedchamber door. "But I look forward to spending the afternoon exclusively in your company."

"As do I."

He hesitated briefly as if considering a kiss. Much to Angelica's disappointment, he took a step back and simply bowed. A cool whisper stroked Angelica's ear. A breeze chilled her skin. She grabbed Randolph's arm before he turned away.

"Do you feel that?"

He frowned even as icy hands brushed the length of her back. She shivered and turned to look, searching for Viscountess Sterling. Frost whitened her breath and worked its way into her lungs. An ache crept over her ribs, tightening her chest until her heart struggled to beat.

"Nothing is out of the ordinary to me, and yet you are clearly freezing." He pulled her into his arms and rubbed his warm hands over her skin. "Where is she, Angelica? Do you see her?"

She shook her head against his chest. "No."

"I'll order a bath for you so you can warm up."

"It's horribly late for that. The servants have enough work to do cleaning up after the ball, and I do think the cold is subsiding a little." She managed not to chatter while saying this last part, lending credence to her words.

"All right." He glanced around. The hallway was empty. "I hate leaving you like this."

"It's all right. I will be fine." She sighed as the cold released its grip and drifted away. "There's not really anything either of us can do until we know more."

"I suppose that is true."

Angelica reached for her door handle.

"Do you know where my bedchamber is?" he asked.

She shook her head.

"Just follow that hallway over there to the right until you reach the door at the end. Fetch me if you need me, no matter the hour."

"Randolph, my mother is right next door and besides, it wouldn't be proper."

"Hang propriety." The command straightened her spine. She blinked and Randolph cursed beneath his breath before adding, "Nothing is of greater importance to me than your safety. Do you understand?"

"Yes. Of course."

He sighed, visibly relieved. "Good." He nodded once as if to confirm that the matter was settled, and strode off with measured steps.

Angelica watched him go before slipping inside her room. But right before she closed the door, she caught sight of Mrs. Essex. The woman stood on the opposite side of the stairwell, as if she'd just come from the gallery. Angelica froze, her breath caught in her throat. Mrs. Essex merely smiled and turned away, leaving Angelica standing in her bedchamber doorway with a thundering heart.

Swallowing, she closed the door and locked it, then went to knock on the door to her mother's bedchamber. "I just wanted to say good night," she told her mother once she granted her entry.

Rose smiled at her with adoration. "Have I told you how happy I am on your behalf?"

Angelica grinned. "At least a dozen times."

Her mother's expression turned serious. "Will you be happy with him if you marry?"

"I believe so. Yes."

"So then the matter that has been troubling you has been put to rest?"

"Not exactly," Angelica confessed, "but we are tackling it together and in the end, I believe all will be well." It was what she had to believe because the idea of being haunted by Lady Sterling's ghost for the rest of her life wasn't one she could accept.

Rose's concern was evident in her tight-knit frown. "Are you certain?"

"Yes." Angelica even managed a smile in an effort to put her at ease.

"Then I wish you a good night as well for I am verily exhausted." She gave Angelica a hug before ushering her back toward her own room. "Your future is brighter than ever before, my darling, and while I know my opinion is biased, I think you will make a splendid viscountess."

"Thank you, Mama."

Rose nodded. "You father would have been incredibly proud."

Angelica's eyes misted and the smile she'd been wearing wobbled a little. She embraced her mother once more before stepping back into her own room. The connecting door closed with a gentle click. Yawning, she rang for a maid to help her undress, then went to work on her hairpins. No more than half an hour later, she was in bed, sinking into blissful oblivion.

AS DIFFICULT AS IT was for Randolph to believe what Angelica told him, he could not dismiss the evidence. For one thing, there was the letter. No one besides him, Katrina, and the person who'd penned it had seen it. He'd made sure of that.

And if that weren't enough, there was the uncommon chill affecting Angelica each time she sensed a presence. He could see it even though he himself was immune.

Standing by the fireplace in his bedchamber, he stared into the leaping flames and wondered why Katrina had chosen Angelica. Because of the room? Because her mind was more open to the impossible? Or because she was the only woman who held his interest?

His skin rippled with sudden unease. What if Katrina was jealous? Her unfaithfulness would suggest she did not care about him or what he did, but what if that wasn't true? Or what if she'd come to punish him for his part in her death? Could a ghost harm a living person and if so, did she have ill will toward Angelica?

Christ, he was going to go mad with all of these unanswerable questions.

A brandy. That was what he needed to calm himself. He'd seen Angelica to her bedchamber. If anything happened during the night, surely her mother would hear.

Somewhat appeased by this rationalization, he poured himself a drink. The ball had gone well and tomorrow he would begin the second part of his courtship. An electric thrill buzzed through him. He could scarcely wait to spend more time with Angelica.

SOMETHING WASN'T RIGHT. She wasn't alone in her bed. In fact... Angelica reached out and touched the warm body beside her. No. This was all wrong. She sat and a lock of red hair fell over her shoulder. Trembling, she stared at her hands in the morning light. An emerald ring gleamed like a frost-covered clover.

Turning, she considered the man who still slept. It was Marcus, the head groom, but what on earth was he doing there and why was he naked? She considered calling Randolph, but hesitated. She remembered nothing from last night's events. What if... Dear God. What if... Her vision blurred only to refocus on a letter. Someone had slipped it under her door and... She remembered Randolph's anger. The words he'd spoken had been unkind – brutal and hateful – but who could blame him? For all he knew she'd betrayed him with Marcus.

A piercing pain cut through her breast. She stared at the letter.

I saw what happened. Meet me at midnight, by the entrance to the east wing if you want my help – a friend.

Of course she wanted help. She loved Randolph and would do anything in her power to make this right – to make him see she was innocent of any wrongdoing. Somebody hateful had obviously gone to great lengths to discredit her in his eyes. But who?

Unsure, she decided to keep the appointment. After all, her bags were already packed. She would be leaving for Fennly House in the morning. Once she did so, her marriage would be as good as over, so what did she have to lose?

The question jarred Angelica's brain as she awoke, startled by the reality of the dream she'd just had. It had been so vivid and clear, she actually found herself searching her bed for the man who'd been in it. Relief steadied her thunderous heartbeats as she came more fully awake and aware of what had transpired. She'd been Lady Sterling again. She'd felt her almost sluggish confusion upon discovering Marcus in her bed and her painful distress later, when Randolph hadn't believed anything she said.

Angelica blinked.

She couldn't dismiss what her recent experience suggested – that maybe the late Lady Sterling had not been the unfaithful wife she had seemed.

THREE DAYS LATER, ANGELICA was having tea outside with her mother and Randolph when he asked if she'd like to take a turn of the garden with him.

"We rarely have the chance to converse in privacy," he said once they'd gone several paces. It was true. Since the other young ladies and their chaperones had departed, Rose was keeping a much more vigilant eye on her daughter. "And I wanted to ask if you've had any more..." he seemed to search for the right word and finally settled on "...encounters."

Angelica shook her head. "No. Not since the dream I mentioned." She'd woken from it in a cool sweat and with deep anxiety due to its tangibility.

"I know this may not be what you wish to hear," she added, "but I've been thinking back on everything I felt during that dream and after – on what I saw and how I reacted. How your wife reacted." Randolph's arm stiffened beneath her hand. Angelica took a deep breath and then ploughed ahead. "Lady Sterling's head wasn't clear and finding Marcus there with her was more than surprising. It made no logical sense."

"She had a few glasses of wine with dinner the evening before. It affected her more than usual, and she eventually claimed a headache, though the truth is she was intoxicated by the time she retired." He cursed beneath his breath, offered a hasty apology and said, "Mrs. Essex later confided that she'd seen my wife and Marcus conversing several days prior in what she described as an inappropriately intimate manner."

Angelica leaned into Randolph's strength and carefully asked, "Why did Mrs. Essex not mention this to you sooner?"

"She chose to approach Katrina instead in an effort to stop any wrongful behavior before it went too far. Her hope was that in doing so, no harm would be done. But it seems Katrina ignored her."

"Even so, I find it unlikely that Marcus would risk his position like that."

Randolph snorted. "He was a groom who caught the eye of a viscountess. As her lover, he probably received all sorts of benefits. And even if he did not, you've seen Katrina's portrait. She was beautiful beyond compare and more than capable of luring any man to her bed."

His words gave Angelica pause. Insight washed over her like ice water. She tugged on her arm and pulled away. "That's why you chose us, isn't it?"

"I beg your pardon?"

"It didn't make sense, your reason for inviting the six most unmarriageable women to your home with the prospect of making one of us your wife." Good lord, she couldn't believe it was only occurring to her now. Most likely because her mind had been too consumed with everything else to give Randolph's reasoning behind his selection much thought. "You want a wife who will not appeal to other men – a woman who has in effect been labeled undesirable."

"Angelica, I can assure you I—"

"Do you deny it?" She knew she was being unreasonable, but the knowledge pricked at her pride.

Having stopped his progress, he turned to look at her so his back was to the house and the spot where Rose still sat.

"No."

His eyes drilled into hers, adding a sense of finality to the blunt word.

"Then I am no more than the best option among the worst."

"Not to me." He suddenly gripped her arm. His mouth became a hard line. A crease appeared on his forehead. "You are the most desirable woman I've ever known and I cannot..." He stared down at her and it seemed he struggled to breathe.

"I cannot stand the thought of you possibly walking away in another few days."

"Why not?"

"Surely the kisses we've shared offer some indication."

"I, um..." If only she hadn't taken their conversation in this awkward direction. She gulped a breath and hastily told him, "My experience with such things is limited."

"As well it should be," he practically growled.

"What I mean," she went on, determined to get her point across before her courage failed her, "is that, given your resolve to convince me to marry you, you could have used the kisses as a ploy with me being none the wiser."

His eyes widened. "Do you honestly think me capable of such trickery?"

"I do not know what to think." Unsure of herself, she forced the words out before she could change her mind. "But I am certain that had we met in London at some grand ball, you would not have looked at me twice."

Randolph muttered something she'd never thought any gentleman would ever dare say in the presence of a lady. He loosened his grip on her arm and slid his hand down to hers. "All things considered, you have every right to be suspicious."

When she kept quiet, he filled the silence while twining his fingers with hers. "My sole purpose was to procure a wife who would give me the heir I require without besmirching my name. So yes, I chose ladies no one else seemed to want because that felt like the safest option. Picking a wife I find attractive was not even something I let myself hope for until you entered the parlor that very first evening and captured my interest."

He raised her hand to his lips for a tender caress. "Since then, you have proven yourself to be more than I ever dreamed possible – a woman whose company I crave with ever increasing intensity."

It wasn't a declaration of love, but it was enough to appease Angelica's concerns and give her some hope. "I feared I might be the only one who was smitten."

The smile that slid into place on his face made his eyes glow like moonlight. "Then I am to understand that you return my regard?"

"I do. Most assuredly."

His smile turned so roguish, her skin started tingling. "I am half tempted to break my own rules and propose straight away." He dropped a look at her as they resumed their progress. "How would you respond to that, I wonder?"

Delighting in the more playful mood they'd managed to find, Angelica told him wryly, "There's only one way for you to find out."

He chuckled, but when he spoke again, his voice was sober. "I would not deny you the last four days you've been given to make your decision. It is a serious, life altering one and, in light of recent events, more complicated than most. I want to be sure you will have no regrets."

In Angelica's heart, her mind was already made up. When the time came, she would accept Randolph's proposal in spite of the drawbacks for one simple reason: she'd fallen in love with the man and could no longer picture her life without him.

Chapter Seven

The days that followed were so perfect Angelica almost allowed herself to forget she'd experienced anything out of the ordinary during her stay at Colchester Hall. With scarcely a cloud in the sky, she'd visited Randolph's tenants two days earlier, bringing baskets of goods she and Rose had prepared. And with the lovely weather persisting, she'd even been able to attend a garden party with him at a neighboring estate yesterday. It was unusually late in the year for such an event, so the guests had all been local, allowing her to become acquainted with the people she'd soon have to associate with on a more regular basis.

Now, sitting adjacent to Randolph at the dining table with her mother directly opposite, Angelica savored the dinner the cook had prepared. It wasn't duck this time, but rather lamb, roasted to perfection, with parsley buttered potatoes and crisp vegetables flavored with spiced oil and vinegar dressing.

Taking a small break from her food, she sipped her wine and listened to Randolph's account of his visit to Rome. He'd gone right after finishing his studies at Cambridge, and he spoke of his travels with so much enthusiasm it made Angelica yearn to see St. Peter's Basilica and the Colosseum for herself.

She sighed. Tomorrow her life would forever be altered. Randolph would offer for her hand and she would accept. Her only regret would be the unsolved mystery surrounding the previous Lady Sterling's death. But with no additional clues to follow, Angelica was at a loss, partly because she'd reached a dead end and also because she was left to wonder why the viscountess's ghost had suddenly chosen to leave her alone when it had been so persistent before.

"Nervous?" Randolph queried once dinner was over and they had adjourned to the parlor. "You've been very quiet all evening."

Rose, who'd suddenly decided she had to keep reading a book she'd begun the day before, had taken a seat at one end of the room while Angelica and Randolph removed themselves to the other. Still within sight, though quite out of earshot. He handed her a glass of sherry and claimed the seat beside her on the sofa.

Angelica sipped the sweet Spanish liquor. Her heart fluttered like mad, as if she and Randolph had only just met and he was making advances. "A little," she confessed.

Twisting sideways to better face her, he caught her gaze with his own. "Then you have made your decision?"

"I made it several days ago and I can assure you it is in your favor." His smile was immediate, warm and happy. "But the nature of it fills me with the sort of trepidation I imagine I would experience right before embarking on a long journey."

"You have nothing to worry about." He moved his leg, just enough for their knees to touch. Angelica's pulse leapt in response. She sucked in a breath. Randolph's smile deepened. "I will be by your side every step of the way."

Angelica carried that assurance with her to bed. And when she slept, her dream was of him. Wrapped in his arms, she savored the press of his lips against hers and the sweet words he whispered against her flushed skin.

Until he drew back and a dark void appeared between them. His face hardened to angry lines. "What have you done?" The words, shouted with hateful disgust, struck her as hard as a fist landing straight in her chest.

It physically hurt. She could feel her heart ripping in two and instinctively reached out toward him only to watch him sink away into darkness. She dropped her gaze to the letter she held in her hand. It was her only hope – the only chance she had left. The floor beneath her turned. Her bedchamber vanished and she was downstairs, dressed in her nightgown and heading toward salvation. A fog clouded her brain. Her movements felt sluggish but she was determined. She rounded the corner and reached for the door. It swung open the moment she touched it. Why wasn't it locked?

Heedless of the wind, she stepped outside and scanned the darkness, but no one was there.

"I hoped you would come."

She spun, so fast she almost tripped over her hem. An elegant figure emerged from the shadows. "Mrs. Essex?"

The housekeeper smiled and glided toward her. "You really should have dressed more appropriately, my lady."

She shivered, hugged her arms around herself, and dug her toes into the ground. Something was wrong. She wasn't thinking clearly. "I ought to get back inside."

"He'll never forgive you, you know."

"What?"

"You've humiliated him in the worst way possible."

"No..." She shook her head. "It isn't true."

"Ah, but who will believe you?" Mrs. Essex's smile sweetened. "After all, there was a naked man in your bed."

"I don't know how...how he came to...to be there." She stepped forward, with sluggish movements. "Please. I must get inside."

"No. You really mustn't."

She blinked. What was the mad woman saying? She couldn't remain out here. She would die, frozen to death. "Mrs. Essex." Gathering all her strength, she bolted forward only to be knocked back by a hard whack to her chest and then to her legs. With a wheeze, she collapsed to the ground. She had no strength and her head wasn't working the way it should.

"You were never good enough for him, and I have finally made him see that," the housekeeper snapped. "Just be grateful for the laudanum. It should help you slip away without too much pain."

Her head tilted back just in time to see the satisfied gleam in Mrs. Essex's ice-blue eyes. Her smile was eerily pleasant, inviting and warm, as she swung the door shut with a thud. The next sound was that of the bolt sliding into place.

"Help me. Please help me."

Angelica's eyes flew open. "Dear God." She bolted out of bed, heedless of the cold swirling around her and the frost sinking into her bones. Her only thought was to tell Randolph what she had learned. It could not wait, it was far too urgent.

Yanking her bedchamber door wide open, she ran out into the hallway. A gust of frigid air followed, propelling her forward. The darkness thickened as she neared the stairs. She paused, giving her breath a chance to claw its way out of her lungs. A chill swept past her ankles, urging her back into motion, only she couldn't quite see and...

A yellow glow slid toward her, pushing the shadows aside like a ship cutting through rough waves. "Lady Angelica?" A face emerged, and a syrupy smile. "Whatever are you doing here at this late hour?"

Angelica's heart spasmed with petrified beats, yet she somehow managed to force a calm tone. "I couldn't sleep. Walking tends to help."

Mrs. Essex tilted her head. "You're breathless." She moved her candle and tried to peer past Angelica. "It seems you were being chased. By one of the grooms, perhaps?" The edge of her mouth curled. "They do tend to like Randolph's women."

A thousand thoughts forced their way to the front of Angelica's mind, each trying to shove past the other in order to gain attention. She decided to focus, not on the familiarity with which Mrs. Essex referred to her master, or on her reference to Marcus, but on the fact that she must suspect Angelica of knowing.

"I don't know what you mean," Angelica tried, hoping to feign ignorance.

The other side of Mrs. Essex's mouth curled. "Are you quite certain?" She narrowed her eyes and leaned a bit closer. "You're shivering." Her chuckle disturbed the air and then she suddenly swung the candle around, illuminating the top of the landing. "Did you do this? Well of course you did. You couldn't just die and stay dead like a normal person, could you?"

Angelica's stomach dropped and she slowly turned. Lady Sterling was there, but unlike the previous time when she'd seen her, her face was contorted into an expression so full of loathing, Angelica gasped.

Mrs. Essex just laughed. "She wishes she had the strength to kill me but—"

Lady Sterling rushed forward. Her arms stretched toward Mrs. Essex's throat but rather than grab her she drifted straight through her on a cold winter breeze.

Mrs. Essex's skirt swayed back and forth in response. She laughed once more. "Well, that was fun."

Angelica stared at her. "What are you talking about?" If she could just make her doubt herself, maybe Angelica could stall for time, or at least make a plan.

"Don't try to pretend you don't know," Mrs. Essex told her playfully.

"Know what?"

"That Lady Sterling is seeking justice." She chuckled. "The poor woman was foolish enough to get herself locked outside in a winter storm dressed only her nightgown. Honestly, whatever did she expect to happen?"

"I have no idea," Angelica whispered. She took a large step back, determined to add some distance. Behind Mrs. Essex, she could see Lady Sterling, looking both helpless and furious.

"In a way, your arrival here is something of a blessing. It doesn't seem fair for her to be trapped here alone with only me for company since I do tend to ignore her." Something distinctly unpleasant flickered behind Mrs. Essex's eyes. "This isn't how I imagined it would be, but now that you're here, I suppose I'll have to improvise. After all, Randolph will never accept his feelings for me if he's always distracted by other women."

"Dear God," Angelica gasped. "You're mad."

Mrs. Essex moved like a cobra, so swift in the dark, Angelica didn't have time to realize her goal before she noticed the flames. Panic engulfed her like never before as she blindly staggered about, patting her nightgown in desperate attempts to put out the fire. An instinctual cry for help worked its way up her throat, until something caught at her ankle. Twisting, she tried to regain her balance, only to find herself falling into...nothing at all.

A peel of amused laughter accompanied her into darkness.

COLD CLAMMINESS WHISPERED across Randolph's skin. "Help her."

The words slid through his mind like morning mist creeping over the moors. Rolling onto his side, he pulled his blanket up and across his shoulders to ward off the chill, but the ice now pricking his toes would not be ignored. It moved up into his feet and his legs and before he knew it, his whole body shook with cold.

"Christ," he muttered, and was startled to see his breath drifting through the air like a puff of white smoke. He exhaled again, then glanced toward the foot of his bed and instantly stiffened. "Katrina?"

Instead of responding, she floated away, vanishing through his bedchamber door. "Help her." The hollow moan breathing next to his ear spurred him into motion. His heart, momentarily paralyzed by disbelief, resumed its rhythm with greater force. He leapt from his bed and flung his robe over his shoulders, shoving his arms through the sleeves and tying the sash as he went.

Christ! The hallway seemed ten times longer than usual, his strides too short to satisfy his need for haste. With a muttered curse he broke into a run, racing toward whatever horror awaited. But nothing prepared him for what he would find when he reached the wide open landing from which the grand marble staircase descended. His heart thrashed about like a trapped bird, and his breaths squeezed tight in his throat, lumping together as he moved toward the railing and peered down into the foyer.

Instinct told him what he would find but the sight of sprawled limbs, charred clothing, and chestnut hair strewn across hard marble sent shivers racing up over his arms and across his back. The hair at the nape of his neck stood on end and his blood froze in his veins. *No*. His stomach twisted as if a rough hand had reached through him to wring out his insides.

Crouched by Angelica's side, Clarkson, his butler, looked up from below. His eyes... Randolph felt time slowing, slipping away and spinning frantically out of control. And then Clarkson said it. "I'm sorry, my lord, but I'm afraid she's dead."

Everything inside Randolph revolted, tearing through him with violent emotion until a choked roar of protest escaped his parched throat. "No. She can't be," he shouted, directing his anger and pain at his butler.

The man merely stared back at him with a wrinkled brow and grey eyes full of regret. Angelica's lifeless body lay at his feet, the spot of blood next to her head like a ghastly signature on a macabre painting.

Randolph started forward. It was like wading through water, yet he knew only one thing and that was he had to reach her. He had to... Dear God, she couldn't be dead. Not when he couldn't imagine a world without her in it, not when he longed for her to tell him she hated his home, his food, hell even his company if that were true. But it wasn't. She'd already told him she wanted to be his wife, and that was what was supposed to happen, not this. Never this. Not when...

His vision blurred and he grabbed hold of the railing, clinging to it for support while his heart started crumbling. He loved her. He loved her so damn much he—

"What's happening? Is everything all right?"

Heaven help him, he'd forgotten about Angelica's mother. He turned, intent on reaching her before she saw, but his feet would not move fast enough and his shaking limbs refused to work as they ought.

"Lady Bloomfield," he tried, "You must not—

But it was too late. Her face came into view, and he saw the moment she registered what must have happened. A wail, so painful it drove through him like a knife, splintered the air. The poor woman nearly collapsed, her legs buckling beneath her until she half hung, half leaned against the edge of the staircase.

"I will bring her to her room." Randolph had no idea how he managed to get the words out, but seeing Lady Bloomfield's suffering told him he had to figure out how to handle the situation someway. He was, after all, the master of Colchester Hall. Angelica had been his guest and...

He swallowed against the knot squeezing his throat.

She should have been so much more.

Slowly, he released his grip on the railing and continued down the stairs. His pace was careful and measured, as if reaching her and confirming her state for himself would make it more real. Ignoring the rapid click of approaching footsteps, he finally knelt by her side and brushed his thumb over her cheek.

"I heard a scream," Mrs. Essex said from somewhere behind him. "Is..." She gasped. "Oh dear lord. What on earth happened?"

Unable to speak, Randolph simply shook his head and scooped Angelica into his arms. The hem of her nightgown was burned all the way to her knees, allowing a glimpse of her ankles and shins which had turned a bright shade of red. Conscious of his stricken servants and her heartbroken mother, he carried her back up the stairs while doing his damnedest to keep himself from falling apart.

"Tell me what I can do to help," Mrs. Essex said. She'd apparently followed him into Angelica's bedchamber and was now hovering near the door while Clarkson lit a couple of oil lamps. The old man chose not to linger once he was done with the task, instead asking Randolph to ring for him if he needed anything else.

Perched on Angelica's bed, Randolph bowed his head over her prostrate body and addressed Mrs. Essex. "Lady Bloomfield will need a stiff drink."

The poor woman had collapsed in a chair and was quietly sobbing away.

"All right, but what about you, my lord?"

He winced in response to the pleasant sound of her voice, so at odds with the mood he was in. "Nothing, at the moment."

"I could stay and watch over her while you and her mother rest."

He closed his eyes, expelled a deep breath. "Perhaps you could—"

Something clutched at the front of his robe, dragging him down until... "Do not leave me alone with her."

The strained words, barely audible as they brushed his face filled his heart with immediate joy and his mind with confusion. "Angelica?"

"Shh..."

Randolph stared at her face, at her fixed expression. Nothing about her suggested she'd spoken and yet he'd heard her. Unless, of course, he was so paralyzed by loss and desperate to have her returned to him that he'd imagined her words.

"Yes?" Mrs. Essex inquired.

"On second thought, I will see to the brandy." He glanced back at his housekeeper, a sliver of unease darting through him at seeing the lack of emotion upon her face. She smiled the moment their eyes met, instantly souring his stomach. "You should return to bed for now. With Lady Angelica's death there will be much for you to do tomorrow."

She hesitated briefly, then nodded and left, shutting the door with an audible click.

Randolph placed his palm against Angelica's cheek. "She's gone. You can open your eyes now."

Dark lashed fluttered ever so lightly against creamy skin. Rosy lips parted and air was sucked in. Angelica squinted against the light from the oil lamps Clarkson had lit. "She...did this." Her voice quivered faintly, but it was enough to draw her mother's attention.

"Is she..?" Lady Bloomfield rushed to the opposite side of Angelica's bed. "How is this possible? Heaven above, I thought you were lost to me, darling." Her hand clutched her daughter's while fresh sobs wracked her hunched form.

"I'm sorry, Mama. I must have..." Angelica blinked in rapid succession, then pulled her hand free from Randolph's and touched the back of her head. The small movement resulted in a painful groan, and when she shifted her weight, her face twisted in agony.

"You took a terrible fall," Lady Bloomfield said. "We have to fetch a physician to look you over right away."

"Not now. Later. I just..." Angelica's words trailed off.

"There's blood at the back of your head." Her mother's voice shook. "You need immediate medical attention."

"I need to speak with Randolph first." Angelica sighed as if speaking was taxing her energy. She took a few breaths before adding, "Alone."

Randolph decided to step in and offer some reassurance before they wasted more time. "I know a good physician, Lady Bloomfield. I'll send for him as soon as I've spoken with Angelica. You have my word."

Lady Bloomfield's lower lip quivered. She sniffed. "All right."

"And please..." Angelica's eyes closed for a brief moment. She winced as she moved her leg. "Stay in your room, Mama. Don't tell anyone I'm alive, just...just drink what Randolph gives you and...try to go back to sleep."

Incredulity widened Lady Bloomfield's eyes, informing Randolph of how impossible sleep would be in her current state. But rather than argue, she turned her attention to him.

"I'll just be a moment," he told Angelica. As reluctant as he was to leave her side, he knew her mother required fortification. As did he, for that matter. Hell, he'd thought he'd lost her, had been so beside himself when Clarkson had said she was dead, he'd not even thought to check for himself.

Returning to his bedchamber, he took a minute to dress, deciding to forego the time consuming effort of putting on a cravat which only threatened to delay his return. He grabbed a bottle of Glenturret and a couple of glasses, then headed back to Angelica's bedchamber.

Relief whipped through him when he found her still there, resting against her pillow with open eyes. His heart eased into a steadier rhythm than it had experienced so far since he'd woken, allowing him to keep a steady hand while filling the glasses. He handed one to Lady Bloomfield.

"Thank you." She took a small sip, licked her lips, and drank again before rising. "If you need anything, please let me know."

"I will see you in the morning, Mama."

Lady Bloomfield nodded and forced a smile. "Very well."

Randolph waited for the connecting door to close before pulling the chair around so it stood right next to the bed. He sat and took Angelica's hand in his. "Would you like some?" He held his glass toward her.

"No. I need to be able to...ugh...think."

"Turn your head a little." Carefully, he helped her move. "Easy. Just like that. Well done."

He parted her matted hair and examined the cut. It wasn't too deep, but it was still bleeding. Grabbing a handkerchief from his pocket he dipped it in his brandy and carefully dabbed at the wound. Angelica hissed in response. Her body tensed, but she let him finish what he was doing without complaint.

When she was resting on her back once more, Randolph gently squeezed her hand. "Tell me what happened."

And as she did, Randolph learned what it truly meant to hate someone, for the anger growing inside him with each word she uttered was worse than what he'd ever felt toward Katrina. This feeling was different. It was dark and gnarly, a deformed creature with twisted limbs, hell-bent on seeking satisfaction. And by God, he'd find it one way or the other. What Mrs. Essex had done to Katrina and to Angelica could not go unpunished.

IT TOOK MORE THAN A week for Angelica to fully recover from her ordeal. After she finished her account of what had transpired, Randolph had woken three footmen: one to guard the door to Mrs. Essex's bedchamber, the second to fetch the local magistrate, and the third to make sure a physician was brought to check on Angelica. The examination had declared her extremely lucky to still be alive considering the nature of her fall and the blow to her head. Her ankles and shins were blistered from the burns she'd sustained, one of her ribs was possibly cracked, and her left hip severely bruised.

According to what her mother had told her, Mrs. Essex had been removed from the premises by the authorities and was now awaiting trial. To this end, the magistrate had interviewed Angelica who'd corroborated the story. Proving Mrs. Essex's involvement in Katrina's death would also be possible with

Marcus's help. Finding the former groom had been a challenge, but after questioning those who'd known him, Randolph had managed to seek him out on a farm a day's ride north of Colchester Hall. And while the young man had initially tried to flee, he eventually agreed to help, provided he could do so anonymously.

Randolph agreed and in the weeks that followed, amidst the increasingly tedious wedding preparations, Angelica did her best to help him recover from the guilt gnawing at his soul.

"Marrying you would make me happier than anything else in the world," he'd told her the evening after her fall. "But I understand if recent events have made you reluctant to choose me as your husband and Colchester Hall as your home."

"That's not a proposal," she'd told him bluntly.

He'd smiled. "Angelica, would you please do me the honor of becoming my wife?"

She'd answered him with a kiss and a whispered, "Yes," against his lips.

"You're sure?" he'd asked while resting his forehead against hers and holding her close.

"Without a doubt," she'd assured him. And then, because she knew how important it was, she'd pulled back enough to meet his gaze with all the love she felt in her heart. "And Colchester Hall isn't nearly as bad as I once suggested."

It was hard to explain, but the misery weighing the old stones down had withdrawn the moment Mrs. Essex was gone. In its place was a light and buoyantly romantic atmosphere, leaving no doubt in Angelica's mind about Katrina finally being at peace.

In the end, they'd decided to take things one day at a time and remain wherever their mood chose. And with all the ensuing wedding preparations, Angelica's slow recuperation, a week-long trip to London, and the legalities surrounding Mrs. Essex's arrest, they'd hardly had time to discuss their future again before their wedding day was upon them.

"I don't think I ever thanked you," Randolph murmured once he and Angelica had retreated upstairs to their private apartment after wishing their wedding guests a good night. Standing near the fireplace with a glass of recently poured champagne in his hand, he watched her intently as she approached. "Had it not been for you..." He shook his head roughly.

With her heart racing against her breast, Angelica set her own glass of champagne on the mantelpiece and stepped closer to her husband. "As I've already told you, you aren't to blame." He opened his mouth as if to protest, but she placed a quick finger against his lips. "However, there is still one thing you should know, and that is how deeply I love you."

His eyes flared with renewed brightness, and champagne sloshed from his glass in his haste to set it aside. Before she knew it she was in his arms, surrendering to the most passionate kiss he'd ever bestowed. Hands slid over her every curve, working buttons and untying ribbons with half-frenzied movements until, quite abruptly, he paused with his face pressed into the curve of her neck. Everything slowed – his progress, her heartbeats, and time. A shuddering breath escaped him, and she felt his hands tremble as he clutched her tight.

"I love you too," he whispered hoarsely against her throat. "More than I could ever hope to describe. And when I believed I'd lost you I... I just knew what I felt for you surpassed all else."

Tears crept along the edges of her eyes until they spilled onto her cheeks. He kissed them away while taking his time to undress her, then kissed his way down the length of her spine, over her hip, and across her stomach until the heartfelt emotions he'd stirred were replaced by intense longing.

"Randolph."

His eyes burned hot as he rose to his feet and stepped back to better assess his handiwork. "God, you're stunning."

A curse followed as he struggled to untie his tricky cravat and again when his fingers slipped on his waistcoat buttons. By the time he swept her into his arms, his body as naked as hers, the tension straining his muscles could not be ignored any more than the nerves clutching her stomach or the heat creeping under her skin.

"So are you," she whispered, because even in this intimate moment, or rather because of it, honesty mattered.

Another kiss increased her yearning for more as he settled her on the bed. His mouth left hers, kissing a sensual path that left no part of her body untouched. Her breaths grew ragged. An insatiable hunger assailed her until she could stand it no more.

"Please," she gasped while he slid one hand up the side of her leg. "Show me what I want, what I need."

A growl shook the air as he settled above her. His dark eyes gleamed. "Have I ever told you—" his mouth burned her skin with another exquisite caress "—how much I adore your boldness?"

"Indeed you have." And just to highlight the point, and also because she was both impatient and curious, she touched him as he'd touched her.

"Bloody hell..." His curse was followed by words of praise, another deep kiss and then finally, blessedly, by the feel of him joining his body with hers. "I love you," he told her once they'd found their shared rhythm. "God, how I love you."

Gripping him hard, she held on tight and followed his lead. "I love you too. Randolph I..."

"Yes." The word hissed between his teeth. "Surrender and let yourself soar."

And so she did, delighting in the sensations he stirred in her heart, body, and soul while relishing the fact that she affected him likewise.

"I've never known anything like this before," she told him later when she was wrapped in his arms.

"I should bloody well hope not," he muttered.

She slapped his shoulder. "You know what I'm trying to say."

"That this was the most exquisite experience ever?"

Turning her head, she touched her lips to his. "Precisely." She reached for his hand and twined their fingers together. "I'm very sorry Katrina died, but I'm glad she led me to you."

When he answered, his voice was hoarse with emotion. "Me too."

Angelica knew he'd loved his wife, and that with everything he'd uncovered, the anger and hatred he'd felt toward her had been replaced by aching regret. But Angelica also knew he loved *her,* so fiercely she had no room for envy or any kind of resentment. For her heart was already full, packed by a love so rich that the only way forward was with a never-ending series of smiles, moments to be cherished, and an endless happily ever after.

Thank you so much for taking the time to read the fifth and final book in my Townsbridge novella series. If you enjoyed *An Unexpected Temptation*, you'll definitely enjoy the first book in the series. Grab your copy of When Love Leads to Scandal to discover how it all began.

If you've already read all the Townsbridge stories you should try one of my other series like The Crawfords where three long lost brothers are reunited when their father dies. Each brother ends up romancing one of three female proprietors of an orphanage, only to realize they've had dire consequences on these women's pasts.

There's also Diamonds in the Rough, a rags to riches series in which one character from each book has to figure out how to navigate high society. Start out with *A Most Unlikely Duke* where a bare-knuckle boxer raised in the slums takes lessons in etiquette from the lady next door.

To find out more about my new releases, backlist deals and giveaways, please sign up for my newsletter here: www.sophiebarnes.com And don't forget to follow me on Facebook for even more updates and fun book related posts and on BookBub for new release alerts and deals.

Once again, I thank you for your interest in my books. Please take a moment to leave a review since this can help other readers discover my stories.

And please continue reading for an excerpt from *When Love Leads to Scandal*.

Acknowledgments

I would like to thank the Killion Group for their incredible help with the editing, formatting and cover design of this book. And to my friends and family, thank you for your constant support. I would be lost without you!

About The Author

B orn in Denmark, Sophie has spent her youth traveling with her parents to wonderful places around the world. She's lived in five different countries, on three different continents, has studied design in Paris and New York, and has a bachelor's degree from Parson's School of design. But most impressive of all - she's been married to the same man three times, in three different countries and in three different dresses.

While living in Africa, Sophie turned to her lifelong passion - writing.

When she's not busy, dreaming up her next romance novel, Sophie enjoys spending time with her family, swimming, cooking, gardening, watching romantic comedies and, of course, reading. She currently lives on the East Coast.

You can contact her through her website at www.sophiebarnes.com

And please consider leaving a review for this book.

Reviews help readers find books, so every review is greatly appreciated!

Don't miss out!

Visit the website below and you can sign up to receive emails whenever Sophie Barnes publishes a new book. There's no charge and no obligation.

https://books2read.com/r/B-A-FJPE-YJLKB

BOOKS 2 READ

Connecting independent readers to independent writers.